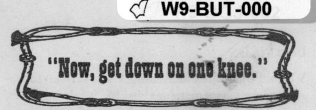
"Now, get down on one knee."

"What are you talking about, Max?" Cisco demanded, bracing himself for the worst.

"Romance, pure and simple," Max said emphatically. "I've decided both you and Gillian need my help picking out a mate."

"Hold on," Cisco interrupted. "Just because you got away with manipulating your niece and nephews into marriages, doesn't mean you can do it to me. Besides," he reasoned, "I'm not even family—I'm only your attorney."

"Don't kid yourself, Cisco. You've become one of us McKendricks, heart and soul, and it's only fair that I give you the same opportunity for happiness that I gave my other three heirs." He paused and continued in his wily way. "I'm not as old as the hills for nothing." Max winked and smoothed his long Lone Star mustache with his finger. "Don't think I didn't notice how attracted you are to Gillian."

Cisco was about to give Max a piece of his mind when Gillian laid down the gauntlet.

"I'm game if you are, cowboy."

Dear Reader,

Wily old Uncle Max McKendrick was sure up to some crazy antics matchmaking his family out there on the Silver Spur Ranch in the first three WILD WEST WEDDINGS books. And you loved him for it! Now he's back—only, this time he's got his sights trained on his faithful attorney, "Cisco" Kidd.

Join Cathy Gillen Thacker as she once again lassos in the sexy cowboys and wacky weddings you've come to expect from WILD WEST WEDDINGS!

If you missed any of the previous WILD WEST WEDDINGS titles—#625 *The Cowboy's Bride*, #629 *The Ranch Stud* and #633 *The Maverick Marriage*, you can order them from the Harlequin Reader Service:
U.S.: 3010 Walden Av., P.O. Box 1325, Buffalo, NY 14269.
Canada: P.O. Box 609, Fort Erie, Ontario, L2A 5X3.

The West was never like this!

Happy reading!

Sincerely,

Debra Matteucci
Senior Editor & Editorial Coordinator
Harlequin
300 East 42nd Street
New York, NY 10017

Cathy Gillen Thacker

SPUR-OF-THE-MOMENT MARRIAGE

Harlequin Books

TORONTO • NEW YORK • LONDON
AMSTERDAM • PARIS • SYDNEY • HAMBURG
STOCKHOLM • ATHENS • TOKYO • MILAN
MADRID • WARSAW • BUDAPEST • AUCKLAND

This book is dedicated to the real Cisco and my dear sister Beth, physicians and newlyweds, who cheerfully—and persistently!—provided the inspiration for the fictional Cisco and his lady love, Gillian. May your marriage be blessed with all the love and happiness this life has to offer.

ISBN 0-373-16697-4

SPUR-OF-THE-MOMENT MARRIAGE

Chapter One

The plan he and Cisco Kidd had executed hadn't been perfect, Montana multimillionaire Max McKendrick decided as he stroked the long Lone Star handles of his snowy white mustache. But the act of faking his own death and putting out an eccentric videotaped will *had* worked in reuniting his three heirs with the loves of their lives. And now five hundred of the most influential people in the West were here to celebrate the triple nuptials right along with him and the rest of the Silver Spur Ranch cowboys.

There were only two things wrong with this picture, Max decided as he surveyed the guests whooping, hollering and kicking up their heels in the festively decorated meadow. Pearl Pendergraph, the owner of the local diner and his lady friend from way back, was still ticked off as heck at him for not confiding his grand matchmaking plans in her, too. And Cisco Kidd, his unofficial "son," was still alone.

Max figured Pearl would get around to forgiving him in time, 'cause he sure as shootin' couldn't imagine his life without her. As for the protégé he had picked up off the mean streets of Butte years ago, brought to the ranch and taken under his wing...well, that was going to be a far sight trickier, Max thought as he downed a shot of whiskey and studied the smart, capable Montana attorney from a distance. Although equally at home in a courtroom or on the ranch, Cisco Kidd had lived a solitary and pricey bachelor's life in town for far too long now. Whether he realized it or not, Cisco needed a woman in his life, ASAP. And, Max thought, grinning, as he began to put part two of his carefully conceived plan into action, he knew— even if Cisco didn't yet—just who that woman should be.

"HONEY, I HATE TO BE the one to tell you, but your dress is buttoned wrong in the back."

A self-conscious flush heated Gillian Taylor's cheeks. "You're kidding," she murmured as Trace and Susannah McKendrick's four rowdy boys went streaking past, shouting hello as they went. She'd baby-sat two of Susannah's boys for years, the whole passel last night during one of the worst storms the area had seen in ages, then spent the day preparing food for the hired hands who'd cleaned up after the storm. She'd been so busy, she'd barely made it to the triple wedding on time, and now, after everyone had said their "I Do's," was still trying to catch her breath.

"Honey, I wish I was joshing you," the owner of

Fort Benton's most popular diner said as she motioned Gillian around.

The flush in Gillian's cheeks deepened as she edged around as directed, practically knocking a vase of long-stemmed yellow roses off a table in the process. "How far off is it?" she asked, juggling a glass of champagne in one hand, and righting the cut-glass vase with the other.

"Well, lift up that gorgeous auburn hair of yours and let me see," Pearl said, pausing to put her own glass aside. "You missed the buttonhole... one...two...three down from the top, and then it continues off all the way down past your waist. I'd say there are about, oh...fifteen or eighteen of those little buttons matched up wrong."

Gillian moaned softly in distress, knowing her dress had been that way through the entire ceremony. "I knew I shouldn't have dressed in such a hurry," Gillian said, still cradling the weight of her wildly curly hair at the nape of her neck.

"Well, never mind that now. Just stand still and let me fix it for you. It'll just take a minute for me to set these buttons to right."

"Thanks, Pearl." Gillian Taylor harnessed her considerable energy as she waited impatiently for Pearl to finish.

Sensing someone watching her, Gillian glanced up, then frowned all the more. That darn Cisco Kidd was staring at her again. She had to get out of here before he tried to talk to her. Fortunately there was a wealth of wedding guests between them, dressed in everything from buckskins and jeans to suits and ties. And all of them, it appeared, wanted to say hi to Cisco before he passed.

"Got dressed in a hurry this evening, hmm?" Pearl continued conversationally as she efficiently unbuttoned and rebuttoned her way down Gillian's spine.

Becoming more impatient, Gillian blew out an exasperated breath. "Pearl, you would not believe the kind of day I've had." And considering the way Max McKendrick's attorney kept trying to approach her, Gillian thought as Cisco continued to close the distance between them, her evening did not look to get any better.

As soon as Gillian's buttons were adjusted, she would say goodbye to the McKendricks and leave. Anything to avoid matching wits and words with Cisco Kidd.

Not that Cisco was bad to look at, especially this evening, with the Montana sun dropping slowly in the sky, giving everything a nice warm glow. Every time she had seen him before, he had been wearing one of his tailored Western business suits and string ties, his trademark bone-colored Stetson and his finely polished hand-crafted boots. Tonight's suit was a dark midnight blue, the shirt a soft complementary medium blue. With the string tie held by a silver clasp around his neck, his cowboy hat tipped back on his head, the six-foot-one-inch, broad-shouldered, slim-hipped lawyer looked as brawny, handsome and rough around the edges as ever.

But as far as trusting him went... Never mind talking to him—that was out of the question, Gillian thought. For one thing, even his name sounded made up. For another, he was too darn nosy. And, worse yet, he was reputed to have as many secrets in his past as she did. Secrets no one but the wily old Max McKendrick had managed to unearth. No, Cisco was not the kind of man she wanted to get involved with, not on any level, Gillian decided firmly.

"Honey, your day can't be any worse than mine," Pearl lamented with an indignant sniff.

Gillian knew Pearl had reason to be upset. Max McKendrick, the eccentric millionaire rancher and Pearl's longtime love, had been thought to be dead until just a little while ago. For nearly a week, Pearl had been in the dark along with everyone else, including Max's niece and two nephews. To Pearl's obvious chagrin, the only person who had known Max was still alive was his attorney, Cisco Kidd. And Cisco had not been talking.

Gillian sighed as Cisco abruptly said something to someone else and headed off in another direction, away from her. "At least we both made it to the wedding," Gillian murmured to Pearl, thinking how glad she was to see the three couples united. Cody and Callie, and Josh and Patience, had married first. Susannah and Trace had arrived late, thinking they'd missed their deadline, imposed by Max McKendrick's will, only to find out they'd never really been divorced! After everyone rejoiced, their four boys had stood up for them as they said their vows again.

Pearl sighed contentedly as she worked on the buttons. "It was pretty romantic, wasn't it, seeing all three of Max's heirs get hitched at one time."

"That it was," Gillian agreed softly. In fact it had been so romantic, it had made her wistful for a man—and an enduring love—of her own.

Abruptly Cisco reappeared at the edge of the crowd. He had a cool, determined look on his face and he was headed her way.

"Listen, Pearl." Gillian tried to wrest free. "I think you've rebuttoned enough."

"Nonsense, honey." Pearl kept a firm grip on Gillian's dress as she buttoned her way down Gillian's spine. "I'm almost finished here—"

"I know, and thank you." Gillian stepped sideways and tripped over the corner of a white folding chair as Cisco disappeared in the crowd of champagne-sipping revelers once again. "But really, I've got to go—" Quickly! Before Cisco could catch up with her and pester her with the questions she knew he'd been wanting to ask.

"Sure about that?" Cisco interjected, popping out around the corner of the party tent to join them. "After all, I wouldn't want you to go around half-buttoned on my account," he drawled with a merry twinkle in his eyes.

Gillian flushed self-consciously. "You needn't

worry about that,'' she said as she hitched in a tremulous breath.

"Good." Cisco appreciatively eyed her long chiffon dress, with the femininely fitted bodice and demure lace collar, before languidly returning his gaze to her face. "'Cause I'd hate to think of you catching cold."

Not likely, with a hot-blooded man like Cisco around. "I don't think we have to worry about that in this June heat," Gillian said dryly. In fact, maybe it was the tiny bit of champagne she'd imbibed before Cisco caught up with her, but she was beginning to feel warm all over.

"Maybe not now, but when the sun goes down, you may need something—"

Or was it someone? Gillian wondered, reading the intense look of masculine interest in his boldly assessing silver-gray eyes.

"—to warm you."

Irritated by the licentious direction of her thoughts—since when did she think of cuddling with a man she barely knew!—Gillian stiffened and folded her arms in front of her. "Thank you. I'll manage."

"I'm sure you will," he agreed.

"Now, if you'll excuse me—" Gillian continued in a low, harried voice.

"You know, Ms. Gillian, you keep this up and I'm going to get the idea you're avoiding me."

Gillian smiled at him sweetly. No doubt about it,

this was one impossible man she was dealing with. "Why would you think that?" she asked.

Cisco shrugged his broad shoulders, but did not take his eyes from her face. "I don't know," he replied, his expression deadpan as he stroked his ruggedly handsome jaw. "Maybe it has something to do with the fact you never return my calls and always seem to disappear the instant you see me coming your way."

So her elusiveness hadn't been lost on him, she realized uncomfortably. "I've been busy," she fibbed, knowing that wasn't what had kept them apart at all.

"Hmm." He studied her with a look that said he suspected she was in trouble, though he could not yet identify what kind.

It was all she could do not to fidget under his knowing look. Cisco was the kind of strong, quietly gallant man she'd always yearned to love. Allowing him to disarm and eventually protect her would be like falling into a thick down mattress at the end of a long day, and having been on the run for nigh on ten years now, the vulnerable part of Gillian longed to surrender herself accordingly. And had she not still had so much to hide, she might've thrown caution to the wind and done just that. But she did have a lot to hide, Gillian realized with a troubled sigh, not only from Cisco but from everyone on the ranch. So all she could do—for now, and for forever—was discourage him.

"You know, sooner or later you're going to have to fess up," Cisco taunted her in a low voice laced with the silky confidence of a man who always, always got his way. "So you might as well just tell me what's got you running scared right now. 'Cause it's highly likely I can use my talents to help you find a legal way out of this jam you seem to be in."

If only that were true, Gillian thought wistfully. But harsh experience had told her this was not so. This situation she was in could only be handled by putting it firmly behind her and forgetting about it, and that was just what she intended to do!

"You know, Cisco—" Gillian changed the subject stubbornly "—if I have been avoiding you, maybe there's a message there."

He grinned at her impudent manner. "One that cuts both ways?"

"Meaning?" Gillian goaded as their eyes clashed.

Cisco smiled and stepped forward so they were standing toe-to-toe. He brushed an errant strand of hair from her cheek and continued to hold her gaze. "That I can be every bit as persistent as you can be elusive. And when I think someone's in trouble, not to mention too damn proud to ask for help when they need it, I gotta tell you, I hang in there like a dog on a bone."

"It's true," Pearl admitted. "Cisco has quite a reputation—as both a Good Samaritan, and with damsels in distress. I don't think there's a woman who's been hurting hereabouts who hasn't cried on his big strong shoulders and benefited from his wealth of legal experience and expertise at least once.''

Unfortunately, Gillian could all too easily imagine not only herself, but a whole stable of other women doing just that!

"So if he's right, honey,'' Pearl continued, patting Gillian's arm gently, "if you do need help—''

Gillian threw up her hands in exasperation. "I do not need help,'' she stated unequivocally. Furthermore, she did not want to talk about this any longer!

Embarrassed color flowing hotly in her cheeks, Gillian pivoted away from Cisco and Pearl. No sooner had she tried to dart past them, than Max McKendrick stepped into her path. The eccentric multimillionaire cowboy-businessman was larger than life and clad in fringed buckskins. And though he might have been as old as the hills, with a leathery suntanned face, he was still as strong as an ox and as sharp as a Montana hawk.

"Well, now, if it isn't Gillian Taylor,'' Max drawled, his silver spurs jangling as he swept off his Stetson to reveal his mane of snowy white hair and a grin as big as all Montana.

"You are just the woman I wanted to see,'' Max announced, taking her gallantly by the arm. "'Cause, darlin', I'd like a word with you.'' Max gestured to include his thirty-something attorney. "Cisco, you and Pearl mosey right along with us,'' Max ordered implacably as he herded all three of them into a white parachute-silk wedding tent.

"Actually, this isn't a good time for me," Gillian said politely as soon as Max had released her.

"Going by past experience, it's never a good time for you," Cisco interrupted.

Max looked from one to the other and stroked his mustache. "I see you two have finally said your how-do's," Max remarked facetiously.

"Not really," Gillian replied, beginning to get a very bad feeling about this.

"We're in the process of getting acquainted," Cisco offered.

Like heck they were, Gillian thought. In fact, if it hadn't been for running into Max, her employer, she would already be long gone.

"I'm mighty glad to hear that," Max said, rubbing his hands together as he regarded them with glee. "Because I have a surprise for each of you."

Cisco Kidd could not imagine what that would be. Max McKendrick's surprises were legendary for both their generosity and outrageous quality. "You don't owe me anything, Max," he told his friend and mentor meaningfully. Max had already given him more than enough, just by giving him a home and family and taking him under his wing all these many years.

Max's leathery face broke into a wide grin. "Oh, I think I owe you quite a bit, Cisco," he remarked with unexpected gentleness. "Without your assistance, I could never've managed to marry off all three of my brother's children to the loves of their lives in one rootin'-tootin' forty-eight-hour period."

"They are happy, aren't they?" Cisco noted, pleased with the way things had turned out.

Max nodded solemnly. "And you should be happy, too," Max said.

Cisco did not trust the sudden mischievous twinkle in Max McKendrick's eyes. It was the same twinkle the rambunctious old cowpoke got in his eyes when he'd talked about his matchmaking plans for Cody, Patience and Trace McKendrick. "What are you talking about?" Cisco demanded impatiently, bracing himself for the worst.

Max slapped his cowboy hat against his knee. "Romance, pure and simple."

At the hint of matchmaking, Cisco noticed Gillian froze and paled considerably.

"There's nothing simple about romance, Max," Gillian interrupted, her thick-lashed emerald green eyes glinting emotionally. "There never has been and never will be."

Ditto there, Cisco thought, agreeing wholeheartedly with the waif-size firebrand with the long, wildly curling auburn hair.

"Which is exactly why I've decided both of you need my help picking out a mate," Max explained.

"Now hold on there a moment Max," Cisco interrupted. He didn't care if the thirty-year-old chef was pretty as could be, with her fair flawless skin, high cheekbones, pert turned-up nose and cover-girl smile. He did not want to be fixed up with anyone via one of Max's grand plans.

"I found the perfect woman for you, Cisco," Max continued. "And the perfect man for you, Gillian."

"I know you may think you have," Gillian sputtered, obviously incensed, the light dusting of pale auburn freckles across her nose standing out against the creamy porcelain of her skin. "But—"

"All you two have to do is agree to a few terms of mine to collect your inheritances and—"

"Inheritances!" Cisco interrupted disbelievingly. As Max's attorney, he had drawn up Max's will. He knew there was nothing in it for him or Gillian. Or at least there hadn't been. And it hadn't mattered to him. Not one whit. It wasn't money or property Cisco wanted from Max. It never had been. He'd thought Max understood that. "Listen to me, Max," Cisco began, working hard to curtail his exasperation with the old man he loved. "You don't need to give me anything—never mind pair me with anyone—when a simple thanks every now and again will do."

"The same goes for me," Gillian added hastily.

Max grinned wryly. "I'll be the judge of what's needed here, you two."

Cisco regarded him in exasperation. "Max, like you, I'm quite happy being a bachelor. Always have been. Always will be."

"And I like being single, too," Gillian said passionately.

Max shrugged, unconcerned, and folded his brawny arms in front of him. "That's what my nephew Cody said, and look at him now."

Obviously, Cisco thought, now that Max was turning over most of his businesses to his heirs, and getting ready to retire, he had far too little to think about these days. "I don't want to enter into a union that is destined to fail," Cisco asserted bluntly.

Max grinned triumphantly. "Trace felt the same reservations about the idea of getting back together with Susannah. He had no faith my idea for fixing his love life would work. But he gave it a chance, and look at him now. Look at them all."

"Susannah and Trace, Cody and Callie, and Patience and Josh are all deliriously happy with each other and their marriages," Cisco agreed.

"But they all had a romantic past with each other," Gillian pointed out, taking Cisco's side. "We don't."

Max grinned, like the wily old whippersnapper he was. "Then it's time we changed that, don't you think?"

DECIDING THE WHOLE McKendrick clan needed to hear the rest, Max rounded them up and brought them inside the tent, too. With arms crossed, he waited until they were all settled in their white folding chairs. "Now, I'm sorry for the interruption, but seeing as how I needed Cisco's help as both an attorney and a matchmaker's assistant the last few days, I could not get to my bequest to him until now." Max pulled up a chair, too, and straddled it backward. "You see, Gillian, I feel partly to blame for Cisco's lack of a wife. I've kept him so busy on the ranch and in the various business deals I've got going on that Cisco here's had no time for romance. But all that is about to change.''

''Look, Max,'' Cisco said shortly as he tossed his hat down on a table and raked both hands through the slightly-too-long layers of his thick dark brown hair. ''What you have done for Patience, Trace and Cody and their spouses is fine, but you don't have to do the same for me,'' Cisco emphasized bluntly. ''I am, after all, only your attorney.''

''Don't kid yourself, Cisco. You've been more than just my attorney for years now. You've become one of us McKendricks, heart and soul, and been like a son to me. That being the case, it's only fair that I give you—and now Gillian, too—the same opportunity for happiness that I gave my other three heirs.''

Max held up a palm to keep them from interrupting. '''Course, I realize your situation with Gillian is a mite different, but I can already see the sparks a-flyin' whenever the two of you look at each other—to the point I know you two are made for each other. So I have decided to lasso you two a chance, and give you two the same forty-eight-hour time period I gave the others for courtship. Only, yours is going to have a twist—''

''Oh, no,'' Cody's wife, Callie, muttered.

''Here it comes,'' Cody agreed.

''I expect the two of you to be married during your courtship. And during this spur-of-the-moment matrimony of yours, the two of you will have to stick to each other like glue, with only three thirty-minute breaks apart. I figure at the end of that time, you'll know in your hearts and souls what I already do—that the two of you are meant to be together for the long haul, too."

"And if we don't agree to this spur-of-the-moment marriage?" Gillian asked, stunned. "Then what?"

"Then I'm afraid the two of you are both going to have to forfeit your inheritances," Max said, nodding at them sadly. "And that is an awful lot to give up. On the other hand, if you marry in the ceremony I have planned for you in just fifteen minutes, at the end of the forty-eight hours, Gillian will receive half ownership in the honeymoon cottage nestled in the trees at the foot of the Silver Ridge Mountains, as well as outright ownership of the Silver Spur logging camp kitchen and dining hall, with a lifelong contract with the ranch to expand her operation to supply meals for all the Silver Spur Ranch crews. Owning this business will give you the financial independence every woman should have," Max said gently. "The cottage—a home."

Neither of which, Gillian thought a tad wistfully, she'd had in a very long time.

"As for Cisco," Max continued, his generosity seeming to have no bounds, "I intend for you to have sole ownership of all my land and businesses and residential properties in Fort Benton, as well as half ownership in the aforementioned honeymoon cottage at Silver Ridge, so that you too will always have a home on the Silver Spur.''

Gillian had only to slant a look at Cisco to know how he secretly longed to have just that.

Max continued in the same blunt, serious manner, ''If, however, the two of you fail to meet the terms I am setting out for you, then you two will share a nontransferable ownership of the honeymoon cottage, but each of you will forfeit the businesses I am leaving you and the security they would bring.'' He smiled at them fondly. ''In either case, the two of you will be bound together for all eternity through your joint ownership of the honeymoon cottage.''

As lovable and outlandish as Max McKendrick was, he was taking far too much for granted, Gillian thought. Especially in pressing them to get married, just fifteen minutes from now! She leaned forward earnestly. ''Max, I know what you've done for your niece and nephews and their respective spouses is nothing short of a miracle. And believe me, no one admires your ability to work matchmaking magic more than me,'' she said softly as she pressed a hand over her heart. ''But Cisco and I do not fall into the same category as the others.''

''Gillian's right, Max,'' Cisco agreed hastily. ''No one appreciates more than I the fact that you're treating me like a member of the family, but Gillian and I can't just get married in fifteen minutes. There are blood tests and waiting periods and licenses to consider—''

"Doc's standing by with the results of the blood tests from the ranch physicals the two of you recently took, and I've been told they'll do just fine. There's a court clerk here ready to issue the license, and the usual waiting time has been waived." Max regarded them, looking very proud of himself. "Anything else bothering the two of you?"

"Yes. We can't stay together for forty-eight hours because we each have to work." Gillian said.

Again, Max smiled in that you-don't-need-to-worry way. "I've prearranged for you both to get time off from work. Gillian, we've got a substitute chef coming in from Butte, starting with the Monday-morning shift. You don't have to worry about tomorrow, 'cause the kitchen's always closed on Sundays anyway. Cisco, your secretary is taking a vacation and attorney Roy McNamara is going to handle anything needing immediate attention, in your absence. So the two of you are all set in that regard, too."

"Seems like Uncle Max has thought of everything," Patience McKendrick commented to Cisco.

"Why am I not surprised?" Cisco muttered, looking every bit as angst-ridden as the rest of his unofficial siblings had been when they'd been unexpectedly roped into Max's matrimonial plans for them.

Max picked up on that, and addressed the issue. "Son, from the moment I met you I believed in you with all my heart, 'cause I knew that you could do anything you set your mind to. I felt the same thing about Gillian." Max held up a hand before either of them could interrupt. "Now, I know it's not going to be easy. Just remember, wanting something is half the battle. Working for it, despite the often-powerful adversities you encounter, is the other half. So when you find happiness, as you two surely will, you need to forget your fears, forget all the reasons why you think this spur-of-the-moment marriage of yours won't work, and reach out with both hands and grab the happiness that is waiting for you. I guarantee if the two of you listen to your hearts, you'll know what to do. Now, Cisco, you get down on one knee and ask Gillian to marry you."

Cisco looked at Gillian and knew there was no way she figured that he would do as Max bid. And he probably wouldn't have, had he been paired with any woman but the elusive Gillian Taylor. Just to get her goat, he took her hand in his and got down on one knee. "Gillian, will you marry me?" he repeated drolly, as the entire McKendrick clan gasped and chortled and whooped with glee.

Gillian blinked, clearly stunned. "I can't believe this," she muttered, looking both confused and incensed. "You're actually proposing?"

"Heck, yes," Cisco acknowledged with mock indignity. "So what do you say?" he asked, bracing himself for the inevitable "No" from Gillian that would end this cockeyed matchmaking plan of Max's once and for all.

Gillian smiled at Cisco ruefully and drew him up off his knees.

"I say...I accept."

Chapter Two

Deciding they were standing much too close, Cisco stepped away from her. He had to have misunderstood. "What did you say?"

"Just what you think I said," Gillian answered, pink color sweeping across her cheeks. "I accept."

"Well, what do you know." Cody McKendrick grinned knowingly as Cisco stood there, shaking his head in wonderment. "Looks like Cisco finally met his match."

"And not a moment too soon," Patience McKendrick added with an amused grin.

To Cisco's chagrin, Max seemed to think so, too.

"I think these two need a moment alone," Max decided. "Tell you what. While you two lovebirds are working out the, uh, details of your union, the rest of us will round up your wedding clothes. When you're ready, give a whistle, and we'll bring 'em to you so you can change before the ceremony."

"Remember now, you've only got fifteen minutes," Trace McKendrick teased.

"Less, if you actually want to be garbed in your wedding clothes at the time you're wed," Susannah added with a wink and a smile.

In unison, Pearl Pendergraph—who'd been suspiciously silent—and the McKendricks exited the tent. Alone, Gillian and Cisco faced off once again.

Gillian tilted her head slightly to the side. "Didn't think I'd say yes, did you?" Gillian said.

Cisco shrugged and tried not to notice how appealing he found the soft, hyacinth scent of Gillian's perfume, or how curvy her petite body was beneath the long, flowing lines of her dress. He drew himself up to his full height and regarded her with a steady, probing gaze. "Why did you?" he questioned.

"Probably the same reason you got down on one knee and asked," Gillian murmured, turning her eyes from his. "To please Max. To join in the fun and be a part of the McKendrick clan, just this once."

"You're telling me you've got wedding fever?" Cisco queried. He, for one, didn't buy it.

Gillian kept her eyes on his a disconcertingly long time, then lifted her pretty chin and regarded him defiantly. "It's a romantic evening."

"So it is."

She blushed at the derision in his low tone. "But you don't think that's all it is."

"No," Cisco said emphatically. "I don't."

"Well, then..." Gillian shrugged and started to walk away.

Cisco clamped a gentle hand on her wrist before

she could even take a step. She might be the most beautiful woman he had ever laid eyes on in his life, and she might have led him on one heck of a merry chase, but this one time she was not running out on him. As she moistened her lips with the tip of her tongue and gave him a droll look, he said softly, "Let's forget about the idea of us getting married for one second here and just cut to the chase, shall we?" With his free hand, he ran his fingers along his jaw. "I've been over your résumé and I know you didn't put forth accurate information—"

Gillian stiffened rebelliously under his bluntly assessing gaze.

"—but I don't know the whole story. That," Cisco continued, leaning in close enough to take in the intoxicating fragrance of her perfume, and the annoyed sparkle in her green eyes, "I can only get from you. 'Cause I figure if you misrepresented certain facts there has to be a very good reason." He released her with that bold declaration.

Her sassy chin lifted. Her eyes, serious and determined, now met his. "I don't know what you're talking about," Gillian replied with a stubbornness that would have been winning if it were not so ill-advised.

Cisco noted the way she was suddenly trembling, and he continued to regard her complacently. "You don't need to fear me because I know something's not right with your life," he said gently.

The flush in Gillian's cheeks deepened. She leveled

him with the angry flash in her eyes. "I don't...fear you."

Well, she sure as heck feared something! Cisco thought, taking in the little jump in her pulse at the base of her throat. "I'm not going to spill anything," Cisco continued.

"Why not," Gillian shot right back, her look turning increasingly mutinous and betrayed, "if you really think I've misrepresented myself to the McKendricks?"

Cisco sighed. Damn, but she was not going to be easy to help out, but he was determined to try anyway. "The fact you've worked side by side with Trace's wife, Susannah, is proof of your excellent character," he explained, letting his gaze drift over her fair, flawless skin and soft lips before returning to her eyes.

"So?"

"So I want to help you," Cisco explained.

"Well, you can't," she told him as she folded her arms tightly beneath her breasts.

Cisco tore his gaze from the soft, womanly curves of her breasts and returned his attention to her upturned face. Eyeing her unhappily, he asked, "How do you know unless you take me into your confidence and let me try? I am an attorney, you know."

Gillian quirked her auburn brow. "Look, I don't know where you get these crazy ideas of yours, but I'm not running from the law, if that's what you think!"

"No one said you were," Cisco replied just as deliberately, aware that just looking at Gillian made his lower body come alive in a way it hadn't in quite some time.

"But there is something that's scaring you—otherwise you wouldn't have that haunted look in your eyes whenever the subject of your past comes up. Otherwise there wouldn't be those discrepancies on your résumé and in what you've told Susannah about your past."

Not wanting his advantage lessened in any way, he held up a hand before she could interrupt. "Yes, you attended chef school at Susannah's behest and cooking classes here and there, but there's no record of you ever attending UCLA twelve years ago."

By now, she looked mad enough to spit nails. "I assure you I attended college," she informed him with a cool haughtiness that would have taken down a lesser man.

"And studied liberal arts," Cisco specified, not about to give up until he got at least a few answers, no matter how feisty she became.

"Yes, although I never earned a degree."

"Then why isn't your name in the university computer?"

Gillian shrugged. "How should I know? Perhaps there was a clerical error."

Silence ticked out between them. Gillian paced back and forth, the skirt of her long feminine dress swirling about her legs. Her arms still clamped firmly beneath the soft swell of her breasts, she continued to regard him warily. "Are you sure you gave the university the right name and Social Security number?" she asked warily, after a moment.

"Positive," Cisco replied.

Gillian turned and looked him straight in the eye. "Then I can't explain it."

"Neither can I," Cisco reiterated softly as he forced himself to forget how sexy and appealing she looked up close, and concentrate instead on her character, or lack thereof. "But I promise you this," he told her deliberately, figuring there was more than one way to skin a mule. "By the time our forty-eight hours together are finished, there aren't going to be any secrets left between us."

This was where she was supposed to either give in to his gentle persuasion and tell all, or say to heck with marriage and run for the hills, Gillian knew. But the honorable Cisco Kidd, attorney-at-law, had another think coming if he thought he was going to dictate her actions so easily!

"Really?" Gillian taunted right back as she continued to regard him with a decidedly cavalier manner. "Then you're going to have to do some fessing up, too."

Cisco's dark brows drew together like thunderclouds. "What's that supposed to mean?" he demanded.

Gillian offered a tight smile. "As soon as you started asking around about me, I started asking around about you," she told him, vaguely aware her voice was rising. "It turns out your past contains more than a hint of mystery, too, Counselor. No one knows where you came from or what your personal history holds, prior to the point where Max brought you to the Silver Spur. All they do know for sure is that you were something of a delinquent when he found you, and that under his tutelage, you became the white knight you are today."

Cisco's lips tightened as he took a step closer. "It's true. Max taught me how to protect and care for a lady—"

"Fortunately for both of us," Gillian interrupted heatedly, "I don't need protecting."

Cisco edged closer yet, a taunting smile on his handsome face. "Sure about that?"

"Positive," Gillian retorted, aware their short amount of time to work things out was swiftly running out. "I can take care of myself. Now, about the inheritances..." Gillian paused and cleared her throat before she met Cisco's eyes and continued matter-of-factly. "Max has held out quite a carrot to us."

"And you want it," Cisco said.

The fact was, for Gillian, that financial security—the funds to literally pick up and run on a moment's notice if need be—would bring her peace of mind in myriad ways. And if she didn't have to run, well, then, she would continue to have a home here. Surely, with the mountain views, deep forests and sparkling meadows...the abundance of land, cut through with the meandering Silver River and the picturesque Silver Lake...there wasn't a more beautiful place to live in all of the world than the McKendricks' vast ranch.

"Don't you?"

Cisco shrugged. "I'm willing to abide by Max's wishes during the next forty-eight hours if you are."

Probably because he thought it'd be easier to unearth her secrets in close proximity, but he was wrong about that, too, Gillian knew. She had thoroughly covered her tracks.

Gillian shrugged and sent Cisco a self-satisfied smile. "Fine. As long as you understand, Cisco, that our spur-of-the-moment marriage is to be strictly a platonic one, because there is no way on this earth I'm falling either into bed, or in love with you, no matter what Max hopes," she told him resolutely. "This is going to be a simple business arrangement, and nothing else."

Cisco did not seem to think that would be the case, but before he had a chance to reply, there was a commotion outside. Gillian swung toward the sound. "What in the world is going on out there?"

"I don't know," he said, concerned, "but I'd like to find out."

Gillian rushed from the tent, Cisco right behind her.

Max and Pearl were facing off on the edge of the dance floor. In his palm Max had a velvet box containing a large diamond necklace, but the obstinate Pearl was refusing to take it.

"Listen to me, you wily old broncobuster! You

have been kicked in the head one too many times if you think I'm going to forgive you for letting me think you were dead!" Pearl was shouting furiously as Cisco and Gillian joined the crowd gathering round.

"Ah, Pearl, come on," Max said in obvious exasperation. He spread his hands wide, pleading his case. "Don't you see? I needed you to really be grieving, for my matchmaking plan to work."

"I do not appreciate being a pawn in one of your games of chance!" Pearl stomped off in a huff.

Max came back toward Gillian and Cisco, looking a little sheepish. "Guess I'm going to have to give her a little time to cool off," he supposed, rubbing the long drooping ends of his white handlebar mustache.

Cisco and Gillian turned to watch Pearl disappear through the crowd. "I don't think I've ever seen Pearl that mad," Cisco murmured.

"Not to worry. She'll see things my way eventually," Max declared with a confident wave of his work-callused hand. That said, he took them in from head to toe. "So, what have you two decided?"

"We've agreed to your terms," Cisco answered matter-of-factly.

Gillian nodded, letting Max know this was indeed so.

Max grinned victoriously, but did not look surprised. He snapped the velvet-lined necklace box closed and replaced it in his pocket, and pulled out another one. "Then you're going to be needing these," Max said as he handed them two matching gold wedding bands.

THANKS TO PEARL and the McKendrick women, a scant five minutes later Gillian was clad in a wedding gown and veil lovelier than anything she had ever dreamed. The air was redolent with the scent of flowers, and the orchestra Max had hired for the now-quadruple wedding was playing a rendition of Pachelbel Canon in D Major.

Gillian floated up the aisle to the white latticework trellis where the ceremony would take place, the bouquet of baby's breath and roses clasped tightly in her hands. It was one of the most beautiful summer evenings she had ever seen, with the stars twinkling above the mountains in an indigo sky. The assembled guests were oohing and aahing over the latest Max-generated excitement taking place, but all Gillian could concentrate on was the ruggedly handsome groom awaiting her.

Cisco was dressed in an elegant black tux, crisply pleated white shirt and black bow tie. Incredible as it was, he looked completely at ease as though he had been waiting for this moment—for her—all his life. As she took her place beside him, he took her hand in his. And then the world fell away as the ceremony began.

"Gillian, do you take Cisco...to have and to hold...for better for worse...for richer for poorer…for the next forty-eight hours…and possibly beyond…?"

Gillian looked at Cisco. "I do."

"Cisco, do you take Gillian as your lawfully wedded wife…?"

Cisco nodded seriously and sounded as if he had a frog in his throat, when he agreed. "I do."

With hands that trembled slightly, they accepted the rings from young Mickey, Trace and Susannah's son, who served as ring bearer for the ceremony, and exchanged the wedding bands Max had given them. And even though Gillian knew this was not a marriage destined to last, the vows were serious enough to make the union feel as if it were going to endure.

The next thing she knew, they'd been pronounced man and wife.

It was done, Gillian thought, feeling almost light-headed with relief. She and Cisco had taken a giant leap of faith, and were actually wed in name only.

"Go on, son," Max urged boisterously as the guests burst into a spontaneous round of applause celebrating their union. "Seal those wedding vows with a real humdinger of a kiss."

Whistles and hollers followed.

Embarrassed beyond belief, Gillian felt a hot flush begin in her neck, move up her throat, into her face, through her cheeks, to her temples.

"Unless you're afraid of what the two of you might feel if you do kiss," Max teased them both with a knowing wink.

The crowd laughed, causing Gillian to flush even more. Cisco gave Gillian a look that literally dared her to acquiesce. "I'm not afraid," she vowed with a lofty toss of her head, aware her heart was already beating wildly in her chest.

"Then that makes two of us, darlin'," Cisco drawled sexily. Regarding her with warm silver-gray eyes, he clamped a strong arm around her waist, and ever so deliberately brought her against him. Threading a hand through the wild, unruly tangle of her hair, he tilted her head back beneath his, lowered his lips to hers and kissed her long and hard and deep, taking her mouth with a thoroughness and an abandon that generated far too much heat, and even more fantasy.

Gillian had never experienced anything like this. Never had her mouth softened so abruptly or her knees gone weak, never had her entire body gone all trembly at just a kiss. But then she had never kissed a man quite like Cisco, either.

She pushed away, stunned at both the shocking intimacy of his kiss and the completeness of her longing to explore the unexpected chemistry between them even more.

It wasn't like her to be so reckless! she thought, dazed and trembling, as flashbulbs went off, and the wedding photographer captured the moment on film for all eternity. It wasn't like her at all!

Darn it, she realized shakily, Cisco was right, this was not going to be anywhere near as simple as they had wished.

THE LAST THING either he or Gillian needed, Cisco decided, as he reluctantly let Gillian go, was to let passion cloud their thinking while she was still in some sort of trouble.

Aware she was already casting a spell over him, a spell he seemed woefully equipped to handle, he struggled to forget the warmth of her lips and the way she had trembled in his arms and melted against him. And instead concentrate on what he did not yet know about her, but wanted very much to find out. One thing was increasingly clear. If he was going to help Gillian, he had to keep his wits about him.

Knowing everyone was still watching them and waiting for the next explosion of romantic fireworks, he gallantly took his new "wife's" arm and led her toward the wooden floor next to the band. As far as he was concerned, the busier they were during the rest of the reception, the better. "Let's dance," he suggested abruptly as he threaded his way through the other revelers to an open spot in the middle.

Still looking a little stunned—from the potent nature of their kiss?—Gillian blinked up at him. "What?"

"Dance." Cisco turned so they were face-to-face, and circled his arm about her waist. In an effort to lighten the tension between them, he looked down at her and explained with mock seriousness, "It's a rhythmic form of moving your body, usually in a pattern of steps, often to the beat of music."

Gillian rolled her eyes and blew out an exasperated breath. "I know what a dance is," she murmured.

"Good," Cisco said, effortlessly taking the lead. "Then let's get to it."

While the other guests all beamed at them from the sidelines, Gillian ever so delicately matched her steps to his. As with their kiss, they seemed a good match from the get-go. As he held her close, Cisco couldn't help but note how soft and womanly she felt in his arms, even if she didn't seem to be enjoying herself all that much. Aware he wanted her full attention—badly—he leaned down to whisper in her ear, "Something on your mind?"

Gillian regarded him with an absent smile. "How'd you guess?"

"Easy." Cisco tightened the hand around her waist. "Care to enlighten me?"

Gillian turned her glance to his and sized him up. For a moment, her breath hitched in her chest. "You'd do just about anything to make Max happy, wouldn't you?"

Cisco shrugged uncomfortably, not sure he liked what she was getting at. "I owe Max a lot."

"Enough to really put on a show for him," Gillian concluded.

Cisco frowned, missed a step or two and loosened his hold on her. "What are you talking about?"

Gillian wrinkled her pert little nose at him and kept dancing to the hopelessly romantic strains of "Love Is All Around." "That kiss you gave me a few minutes ago,'' she replied dryly as the wedding photographer came by and snapped their photo again.

Cisco stiffened, very much aware his lower body was still throbbing hotly from the unexpected fireworks of their embrace. ''What about that kiss?'' he demanded gruffly, trying not to notice how pretty she looked in the white lace-and-satin wedding dress, or recall how soft and giving she had been as she melted in his arms.

If he wasn't careful, he'd end up thinking she was his real—and not just temporary—bride.

Gillian tossed her head. Silky auburn curls flew in every direction. ''I let you get away with it this time because you caught me off guard. Don't expect me to cooperate with your attempts to show off again,'' she said in a low, sexy voice only he could hear.

''That's what you think our kiss was about?'' Cisco asked, annoyed she accused him of feigning the passion he'd felt. *''Showing off?''*

Gillian gave him a look that said, *What else could it have been?* Then she answered, ''Yes,'' as twin spots of color swept into her cheeks. ''And as you have now seen for yourself, I can put on a show just as well as the next person.''

She sure had, Cisco thought. He'd been completely taken in by the starry-eyed way she had gazed up at him and trembled in his arms. He'd thought the impact of their postwedding kiss had affected her as much as it had him. Boy, had he been wrong, he thought as the song ended to a lot of hooting and hollering and once again the floor filled with other couples.

Gillian studied him, a perplexed look in her eyes. "I thought that was what you—and Max—would've wanted," she murmured as the two of them began two-stepping to the strains of "Boomerang Love."

"You're right," Cisco countered, telling himself the last thing he needed to do was lose his heart to this vixen in white. "It is," he said, giving her the slow, casual once-over. "And now that we've done our duty, I say enough of the dancing." And anything else halfway romantic, he amended silently. "It's time for a glass of champagne." Taking Gillian's elbow, Cisco guided them to the edge of the dance floor, and from there, slipped through the crowd. They'd almost made it to one of the white-coated waiters, when a pleasant-looking man with short brown hair and friendly brown eyes intercepted them. "Hey, Cisco."

"Hey, Pete." Cisco shook hands with the fellow in the lightweight tweed sport coat. Cisco grabbed two glasses of champagne from a passing tray, handed them both one and got a third for himself. "Have you met Pete Lloyd?" Cisco asked Gillian.

"That's just what I was trying to figure out." Pete smiled at Gillian as he sipped his champagne. "I don't want it to sound like I'm laying a line on you, but I have the oddest feeling we know each other. I just can't remember how."

Gillian flushed and looked vaguely uncomfortable

to be put on the spot that way. "Actually, I don't think we have met." She paused and bit her lip, then, still studying Pete, continued, "At least you don't look at all familiar to me. Maybe we've seen each other in passing here on the ranch somewhere, or in the logging camp kitchen where I work."

Pete mulled that over as he sipped his champagne. "I suppose that's possible. I was last at the ranch three months ago—"

Gillian cut Pete off with a shake of her head. "I didn't work or live here then."

"Perhaps in Fort Benton, then," Pete suggested.

"Maybe. I've been in town a number of times since I moved here three weeks ago," Gillian admitted.

"But I haven't." Pete frowned. "I just arrived in Montana a week ago, and I spent the whole time getting settled in Missoula."

"Pete's recently accepted a position teaching cattle-management courses at the University of Montana," Cisco explained. "Prior to that he taught at Kansas State University."

Abruptly, a little of the color faded from Gillian's face. "Really," Gillian murmured, for a moment looking a little like a deer caught in a vehicle's headlights. "How did you get to know Max, then?" she asked around a sip of champagne.

Pete smiled as the wedding orchestra struck up yet another romantic, lively tune for the two-stepping crowd. "Max and I share the same theories when it comes to herd management and crossbreeding cattle.

We've corresponded regularly over the years and Max has recently agreed to underwrite a work-study program for the Ag department at the University of Montana.''

"Pete's going to be in charge of administering that. So you'll be seeing him a lot here," Cisco said.

Pete nodded. "Starting next week, I'll be here most of the summer working out the details."

Gillian paled a little more. "Congratulations," she said, albeit a little hoarsely.

Pete grinned back. "Thanks." He paused to take a closer look at Gillian, as did Cisco. "Say, are you all right?"

"You are looking a little pale," Cisco agreed.

"A little too much excitement for one evening," Gillian said, passing over the glass of champagne. She looked at Cisco. "Perhaps if we took a break from the festivities—?"

"Sure thing."

"Nice to meet you," Pete said.

Gillian smiled at Pete. "The pleasure was all mine."

His arm wrapped protectively around her waist, Cisco led Gillian through the crowd. "You sure you're okay?"

"Yes. Absolutely. I just—I meant what I said about taking a break from the festivities. In fact, if it'd be okay with you, I really want to leave the reception as soon as possible."

Cisco did a double take. "Now? The party's not

quite fully under way.'' Knowing Max—and the rest of the McKendricks—the whooping it up would probably go on 'til dawn.

"I know, but I've got some business to attend to back at the logging camp kitchen,'' she said coolly.

Although he had known from the get-go they would not make love, or come anywhere close to it during their spur-of-the-moment matrimony, this was not what Cisco had expected from her on their ''wedding night.'' Furthermore, he couldn't imagine what she had to do since Max had arranged for them both to have time off.

"What I have to do there is probably going to take more than a few minutes,'' Gillian continued, her chin set with customary stubbornness, ''but if you want to take our first break apart now, and meet me there in thirty minutes, it's fine with me.''

And let her ditch him already? Especially after that odd run-in with Pete Lloyd? Cisco didn't even have to think about the options. "No, I'll go with you.''

"You're sure now?'' Gillian replied, looking as though she wanted more than anything for him to change his mind.

Which in turn made him all the more certain she was running from something or someone. It was up to him to figure out what or who that was, and then fix things via legal means so she would never have anything to fear again.

"Positive,'' Cisco said with a firm smile, the protectiveness he felt for the vulnerable woman in front of him growing as swiftly as his mystification. "Where you go, I go. That's the way Max wants it, at least for the next forty-eight hours, and that's the way it's going to be."

Chapter Three

"You're awfully quiet," Cisco noted as he parked his
luxury sports car in front of the logging camp dining
hall and cut the motor.

And then some, Gillian knew as she worked the
veil and tiara out of her hair and laid them across the
back seat. She'd barely said two words to Cisco since
they had slipped away from the wedding reception,
ducking out on, among other things, the buffet dinner,
the bouquet toss, the garter removal and the cake cut-
ting.

Her only regret was that they'd been unable to
quickly and quietly find the clothes they'd had on
before the wedding. So, rather than risk detection—
and possible delay, they'd given up and fled as they
were, in wedding gown and tux.

But the trade-off was worth it, she figured. If they'd
stayed at the celebration much longer, she might've
begun to feel as though she really had gotten married
tonight. And that, as she well knew, was ridiculous!
She and Cisco barely knew each other. Plus, they

were only in this for reasons that had nothing to do with the love that should exist between two married people. She wanted—needed—a new but legal identity, a family and a home to call her own. And if she went through with this, she would have all that. Whereas Cisco wanted to please—and placate—the always-far-too-generous Max as well as prove he was every bit as adventurous as the other McKendrick men.

Of course, Gillian thought wryly, aware her heart was still beating too fast, and had been since their vows had been exchanged, she and Cisco still had to convince Max they were all wrong for each other. The only way she and Cisco could possibly do that was to literally show him that they were most definitely not a match made in heaven! There was no better time to do that than in the next forty-six hours. She just hoped the process of demonstrating their incompatibility would not prove too painful for either of them.

"You feeling okay?" Cisco continued as he shot her yet another quietly concerned look.

Gillian nodded and tried not to notice how much of the interior of the car his broad shoulders and tall, brawny frame took up. "I've just got a lot on my mind," she confided as she turned her attention to the logging camp dining hall. The large square building was out in the middle of nowhere and surrounded by dense, forbidding woods that might have unnerved her if the parking lot had not been lit by soft yellow lights that illuminated the area with a peaceful, romantic glow.

Cisco shot Gillian an interested glance. What lay ahead of them was a challenge. They both knew it, understood it. "I guess you do have a lot to think about," he murmured. As inherently gallant as ever, he circled around to open her door and put out a hand to help her out of the car. "Figure out yet how Pete Lloyd knew you?" he asked casually as he took her hand, assisting her from the passenger seat.

No, Gillian thought, as her pulse picked up another notch and a guilty flush flowed into her cheeks. *But I have a good idea how it might've happened.* And that, in turn, could lead to trouble if Pete ever put two and two together. Cisco was still waiting for an answer, but she didn't dare tell him anything but a smidgen of the truth. Knowing this was one question she was not going to be able to duck, she paused to look at Cisco and spoke as much of the truth as she could. "Pete's a very nice man, but he's mistaken. The two of us have never met."

A skeptical look on his face, Cisco released Gillian's hand. He then thrust both hands in the front pockets of his tuxedo trousers as he strolled by her side up the front walk. At the entrance to the dining hall, he braced a shoulder against the doorframe and watched as Gillian used her keys to unlock the door. His shoulders and chest looked hard and sinewy beneath the handsome tuxedo jacket. "You've never been to Kansas, then?"

Wishing he didn't look so sexy with the moonlight glinting off his dark hair, Gillian shrugged and opened the door to the dining hall. "Another lifetime ago, maybe," she murmured absently.

Simmering with frustration, Cisco gave her a narrow glance. "What does that mean?" he demanded as he followed Gillian into the hall and watched as she routinely switched on the lights.

"That I don't have either the time or the inclination for your third degree, Cisco." Her skirt swishing softly as she moved, Gillian swept past the adjacent kitchen and storeroom containing pantry shelves, commercial refrigerator and freezer.

Aware he was right behind her, she moved briskly through the vast dining hall, to the cafeteria office. "And you are about to see why," Gillian finished autocratically as she flipped on the last set of lights.

Cisco stared in amazement at the heavy tree limb, surrounded by a circle of broken glass, jutting into the center of the room. A bookcase filled with cookbooks had been upended. Glass fragments, bits of bark and leaves and what was left of the miniblinds that had once covered the window lay scattered across the desk, file cabinets and tile floor.

"This happen in the storm last night?" Cisco guessed, already righting the bookshelves for her.

Gillian nodded. The worst thunderstorm the area had seen in ages had knocked out power and phone lines, caused a flash flood of the Silver River and the loss of one of the horse barns to fire. She shoved her hands through her hair and released a beleaguered sigh. "It was this way when I got here midmorning," she said, already picking up several cookbooks that had been knocked to the floor, carefully reshelving them in the specific order she wanted—general cookbooks in one place, low-cal in another.

Cisco didn't have to ask why it hadn't been cleaned up yet. He knew as well as she the ranch crews had been stretched thin trying to attend to all the storm-generated calamities, in order of importance, and prepare for the huge wedding celebration Max had arranged.

He picked up several cookbooks and handed them to her one at a time.

"I would have tended to this whole mess earlier," Gillian continued, carefully checking and sorting each title before she put it away, "but because the roads were practically impassable, I was the only person able to get here today. And once here, I had my hands full trying to make coffee and sandwiches to take out to the crews. I worked right up 'til the time I was due for the wedding, which I didn't want to miss for obvious reasons." And then had dressed in such a mad rush, she'd arrived with the back of her dress buttoned all wrong. "But now I'm back where I left off." Gillian sighed and shook her head as she finished reshelving the cookbooks.

And the destruction was so overwhelming, she barely knew where to start, Gillian thought as she turned to study the long jagged splinters of bark, scattered twigs and leafy green leaves, and dangerously sharp glass shards.

"Let me give you a hand with the rest of this," Cisco said.

Though she would've welcomed the aid under other circumstances, Gillian did not want to be any more beholden to Cisco than absolutely necessary when this was all over. It was enough she was accepting the inheritance from Max.

She turned to Cisco as she slipped on a heavy white waist-to-knee chef's apron over her wedding dress and tied it snugly around her waist. "Thanks, but I think I can handle the rest of this myself," she said casually, knowing by the faint darkening of his irises she had irked him with what some men had referred to as her damnable independence. "There's no need to mess up your tuxedo."

Cisco folded his arms in front of him and raked her with a glance that had heat pouring through every inch of her. "What about your dress?"

Gillian shrugged, no more willing than him to be dissuaded. "I admit it's not my choice of work garments, but it's no more awkward than some of the themed costumes I used to wear when I worked for a catering service years ago." Back then she'd cooked and served in everything from full medieval dress to a pumpkin costume. "Besides, I doubt I'll ever be wearing this dress again."

"And meantime you don't want to take time to go back to your quarters and change," he guessed.

Gillian nodded in the affirmative. "You read that right." She felt she had already wasted enough time in taking care of this. Because in the end this business was going to be what mattered to her most.

Cisco made a show of studying the offending tree limb, some six inches in diameter and fifteen feet long. "You're sure you don't want my assistance?" he asked with a look that said she was going to be sorry if she didn't accept his gentlemanly offer of aid.

"Positive." Gillian forced a polite smile. "Thanks anyway."

Cisco shrugged his broad shoulders laconically. "Suit yourself." He pulled up a chair from the adjacent dining hall, placed it just inside the office doorway and sank into it backward, his long legs straddling the seat.

Gillian's green eyes widened in surprise. Since he was clearly not needed here, she had expected him to busy himself elsewhere. Not stay underfoot. "What are you doing?" she demanded, forcing herself to meet his subtly challenging gaze.

"Watching." Cisco unknotted his black bow tie and unbuttoned the first two buttons on his shirt. "Unless I miss my guess—" his silver-gray eyes gleamed as he flashed her a sexy grin "—this ought to be quite a show."

As Cisco had hoped, his words immediately had the desired effect. Unable to thoroughly and promptly discount him, as she had obviously hoped to be able to do, Gillian whirled back around, muttering something he couldn't quite catch but was quite sure was derogatory anyway.

"Singing my praises again?" Cisco teased, eager to see how she planned to accomplish this alone. If anything was likely to yield a few easy clues about her, and give him ideas how to help her out whether she wanted him to or not, it was spending time together. And thanks to Max, with the exception of their three short thirty-minute breaks, during the forty-eight-hour period they wouldn't be doing anything but sticking to each other like glue.

"You just *wish* I was singing your praises, Counselor," Gillian responded temperamentally as she caught the flowing skirt of her wedding dress in both hands, gathered it over her apron, just above the knee and—to his complete surprise—tied the ends in a staying bow just above her knees.

Her freedom of movement thusly assured, she knelt down to pick up large triangles of broken glass and lay them in the metal waste can. Once those were out of the way, she also moved the swivel chair that went with the desk.

"Okay, here goes," she said.

She lifted both arms above her head. The motion lifted the fitted lace and satin bodice of her high-necked dress against the soft jutting curves of her breasts. Cisco watched as Gillian wrapped both hands around the six-inch-thick limb and pushed. And pushed. And pushed.

"Far as I can see, that limb did not move at all,"

Cisco pointed out dryly, forcing himself to ignore the way each gargantuan effort caused her breasts to lift and lower with delicious abandon.

"That's because the other end of the limb is stuck in the mud outside." Gillian scooted the chair over, climbed on the desk, the higher vantage point putting her just about on par with the high-cut office window, and giving him a spectacular view of her shapely, stocking-clad legs.

Leaning over, she peered at the ground below. Looking at the alluring curve of her slender hips, it was all Cisco could do to suppress a groan. "Ready to give up yet?" he asked, knowing he couldn't sit idly by and watch much more of this.

"Not on your life," Gillian tossed back, her soft lips pursed together thoughtfully. "I'll just try this—" She marched militantly back down from the desk and, still being careful not to mess up the dress she was wearing, wrapped both hands around the top of the branch and tried to pull the protruding end of the limb down so it would lay levelly across the windowsill.

"And—" She continued to huff and puff in obvious frustration. To no avail. The limb did not budge.

If it was this hard to get her to accept help on something this mundane, what would it be like to get her to take his help on something really important? Cisco wondered.

"What about now?" he queried dryly, folding his arms across the ladder-back of the chair.

"Nope," Gillian retorted with a determined scowl. She moved this way and that as she tried to find a position that would give her better leverage. Finally finding a place to her liking, she drew a deep breath, swiveled her hips like a golfer preparing for a shot, relaxed her upper body with a similar sinuous wiggle and lifted her arms once again. Her efforts nearly pulled her off her feet, but did nothing to so much as budge the heavy limb, never mind give her the leverage she needed to move it out of the building. Stepping back to reevaluate, she released an exasperated breath and frowned.

"We could just leave it where it is," Cisco offered, turning his head slightly to the side as he studied the offending branch. "It might make a nice coatrack. Though I dare say it'd get a little chilly in the winter, what with the cold Montana wind whipping through and all."

His facetious suggestion was rewarded with a temperamental flash of her emerald green eyes. "Don't you have something better to do?" Gillian snapped.

Enjoying the twin spots of color in her pretty cheeks, Cisco shrugged and kept his eyes on hers. "Can't think of a thing."

Gillian's luscious lips thinned into a belligerent line. "Have it your own way, then."

Pausing only long enough to exchange her heels for a pair of tennis shoes, she strode past him, snatched up a flashlight and a large serving spoon from the kitchen, headed out the back door, around the building and into the dark.

Curious to see what she was up to next, Cisco followed her and watched as she squatted next to the splintery end of the fallen branch and began to dig a trench in the mud around it. Finished, she tried to lift the limb again, to no avail.

Cisco figured they'd done things her way long enough.

Afraid she was going to strain her back if she kept it up, he caught her hands and brought her to him before she could lift again. "C'mon, now. Let me help you before you hurt yourself," he urged softly.

She glared at him, her wrists trembling in his staying grip. "I told you I don't need your help."

"Don't need it, or are afraid to take it for fear you might then be relying on someone other than yourself?" Cisco questioned as her breasts rose and fell with every agitated breath.

"And I don't want you dogging my every step," she said, shaking free from his hold.

Grabbing her flashlight, she cleaned the mud off her shoes as best she could and stomped back inside, Cisco close behind. Across the dining hall. To the office. Once there, she climbed back onto the desk, lifted a leg, and to his growing amazement, swung it over the log so she was seated atop it seesaw fashion.

Realizing her behavior had taken a dangerous turn, Cisco gave her a narrow, warning glance. "That is not going to work," he told her flatly. In fact, he was sure of it.

"I'll be the judge of that," Gillian tossed back haughtily. Ignoring his warning, she pushed up with her tocs, then down again as hard as she could.

The log shifted slightly, all right, just enough to throw her off balance. Gillian gasped as the slippery soles of her shoes slid across the surface of the desk.

Braced for just such a calamity, Cisco stepped forward, arms outstretched just as Gillian lost her grip on the branch, went flying backward and landed in his arms. Holding her dainty weight against his chest, he tightened his grip on the headstrong waif who was now his bride. "Now do you want my help?" he asked softly, looking down at her and wondering what it would take to get her to rely on him just a little bit.

Gillian bit her lip as he slowly righted her and lowered her gently back down to the ground. "Maybe I—"

"*We* can do this if we work together." In fact, they could accomplish a lot of things if they trusted each other—even a little bit.

Gillian flushed in embarrassment. "Fine. Have it your way, then."

"Thanks. I will." Ignoring the way she rolled her eyes at him in response, he positioned her at one end of the fallen limb and, after shrugging out of his tuxedo jacket and rolling up the sleeves on his heavily starched white shirt, took his place closest to the broken-out window. "When I say three, pull down toward you,'' Cisco instructed. ''Okay. One, two, three...''

The branch shifted with a groan. Cisco pulled down until the opposite end was up and out of the mud; then, with the branch still balanced on the windowsill, he began to push. As he had predicted, five minutes later, they had the branch clear of the windowsill. It hit the ground with a satisfying thunk that had them both smiling.

''Thanks,'' Gillian said, dusting off her hands and looking pleased despite herself. ''You can make yourself comfortable while I clean up the rest.'' Her manner brisk, she started to brush by him.

He caught her arm, pulling her to a stop. Her stubbornness was costing them both a lot of time, and he for one did not want to be here all night. But she apparently did. For fear they'd be tempted to share another kiss?

Pushing that possibility—and other even sexier options—out of his mind, he focused firmly on the task at hand, correcting, ''I'll pick up the glass. You go see if you can't find some cardboard to tape over the window.''

She reacted as gratefully as he had expected. ''I don't think we've got any.''

She was not getting rid of him until he had accomplished what he'd set out to do, and sooner or later she would realize that. ''What do you have?''

She took a minute to think about it. ''Some heavy-duty garbage bags.''

"Then that'll have to do. Won't it?"

She held his glance, her expression gradually accepting but no less mutinous. "I suppose it will," she murmured eventually, then spun around and left in a drift of hyacinth perfume.

Cisco watched her until she disappeared from sight, before he started carefully picking up debris.

He knew Max was counting on him to find a way to help Gillian out of whatever jam she was in, and perhaps find a little romance in the bargain. The first task was going to be a lot easier than the second, but he hoped he could manage, because Gillian was clearly hiding something. Not just from him, but from all the McKendricks. And that *something* had her running scared.

DARN IT ALL, Gillian fumed. She didn't care what he did. She was not going to let Cisco Kidd get to her. Gillian swept purposefully toward the dining hall kitchen for plastic to cover the broken window for the night. Not that he wasn't trying his damnedest to get under her skin. Being frankly suspicious of her every avowed statement one moment, then incredibly, playfully, helpful to her the next. She had no doubt he wanted to use their enforced proximity to each other during the next forty-five-plus hours to snoop even further into her private life, but he had another think coming if he thought she was going to tell him anything. She was a solo act all the way these days and she planned to stay that way.

Fortunately, they had a lot to keep them busy, even if it was technically supposed to be their "wedding night."

Aware it was getting late, she rummaged around the kitchen, lamenting the lack of organization all the while. Biscuits, the previous cook, had left it in terrible shape. Nothing was stored where it should be. He had silverware tucked next to the canned peas, plastic storage containers next to the self-rising flour. From the moment she'd set eyes on the spacious work area, she had wanted to organize it properly. Now, having learned of Max's plans to give the dining hall to her outright once the forty-eight hours were up, she wanted to get her hands on it twice as bad. But she supposed, as she reached for the roll of plastic garbage bags on the shelf above the sink, it would have to wait until tomorrow, or the day after, since she doubted she could get Cisco to remain here with her while she worked nonstop.

Without warning, a chill moved over her, so cold it made her hair stand on end. Whirling, Gillian looked around her and saw nothing out of place. She drew a deep breath and told herself she was being ridiculous. No one was here. No one was watching her. She was just letting Cisco's suspicions that her past was not as far behind as she liked to think and the unexpected run-in with Pete Lloyd get to her.

Not that she really had anything to worry about there, either. It had been such a long time. She might look familiar to him, but what she'd told Cisco was true, she and Pete had never met. Chances were excellent Pete was never going to recall anything. Hence, all she had to do now was calm down, concentrate on the tasks at hand.

That agenda in mind, she took four black plastic garbage bags off the roll. And that was when she felt it again—the sharp unmistakable sensation of being watched. And there was only one person here tonight in the dining hall who could be spying on her, she thought, her temper soaring.

"Cisco?"

"What?" His voice sounded both muffled and far off.

So it wasn't him. Gillian looked around and tried to get a grip on her jangled nerves. "Can I bring you anything?" she yelled back, aware her hands were trembling as she searched the utility drawer for a pair of scissors and a roll of tape.

"A dustpan and broom would help," he called from the other end of the building. "Did you find what you needed?"

"I'm still looking!" Gillian shouted as shivers continued to ghost down her spine. Finding neither scissors nor tape, she shut the utility drawer in frustration and headed for the pantry. She was almost to the doorway when a can tumbled from the shelf, rolled out onto the center of the kitchen floor and landed at her feet.

There was no reason for her to freak out, Gillian

told herself firmly. Sometimes things were not set right on a shelf.

Taking a deep breath, she continued moving forward. As she passed through the open portal, a second can bounced off the shelf and tumbled toward her. Her heart pounding, Gillian whirled toward the shelves of canned goods. There was nothing out of place that she could see, nor did there appear to be anyone in here. Nevertheless, she backed swiftly out of the pantry and did a quick check behind her.

The rear door to the kitchen was closed and locked. The windows were still intact, despite the storm, the one to the right locked, the one to the left...open. Her heart sinking at the oversight—for she knew she had forgotten to close and lock it before she went to the wedding—Gillian moved toward it. Her knees trembling, she realized anyone could have removed and replaced the screen from either the inside or the outside with no one being the wiser.

Angry she'd made such a crucial mistake, when—if not for Max and his matchmaking—she would have been coming back here alone after the wedding, Gillian reached up to pull down the bottom window. It snapped into place with a satisfying thud that soon had her sagging with relief.

Everything was fine now, she reassured herself firmly as she swiftly turned the lock. Those cans had probably been knocked off the shelf by the breeze blowing through the open window.

Or had they?

CISCO DIDN'T KNOW *what* came first—the cacophony of noise, the tremendous crash or Gillian's high-pitched, absolutely terrified shriek. He only knew, as he sprinted across the dining hall to the kitchen, he had to get there fast.

Hand pressed to her mouth, Gillian came tumbling out of the pantry and smashed—backward—into his chest, a fact that only made her jump in surprise and shriek all the more. "For God's sake, what is it?" Cisco asked above her muffled gasps, holding her close.

Trembling, Gillian could only point.

Cisco looked down. At the back of the long walk-in pantry, a mother raccoon and four baby raccoons were poised for both fight and flight.

They had probably found their way in through the broken window via the downed tree branch, looking for shelter after the storm, and had then taken up residence in the pantry.

But Gillian, a real city girl, obviously didn't know that, Cisco thought, amused. "It's all right," Cisco said, using his grip on Gillian's arms to shift her protectively behind him. "They're probably more scared than dangerous, and just want a way back outside."

"Then they should have asked for directions!"

"I'll tell them to do so next time." Cisco turned to face her. "You going to be okay if I let you go?" She felt so good all cuddled up against him, he was tempted to keep right on holding her like this.

"Of course!" She put a palm to his chest and pushed him aside.

His eyes still drifting over her, he made his way to the back door. He opened it wide, securing it so it would stay open, then moved back in the opposite direction.

The mama raccoon sized them up carefully, then led her babies, one by one, out the back door. Cisco waited until they were gone before he shut the door again, locked it and turned back to Gillian.

To his surprise, she still looked as though she was going to jump out of her skin. For reasons that seemed to have little or nothing to do with the raccoons.

He filed away the worrisome bit of information for future reference, then stepped forward and took her in his arms once again. "You can stop shaking now," he said.

That, Gillian thought, as she relaxed in the warm and comforting circle of Cisco's arms, was a task easier said than done. The feeling of being watched had triggered an onslaught of unpleasant memories, and try as she might, even with Cisco watching her intently, she couldn't seem to stem the tide.

Her whole body stiffened in annoyance. "I'm trying, believe me," Gillian replied.

Cisco gently brushed a strand of hair from her face and continued to study her intently. She had no idea what conclusions he was drawing from all this and was sure she did not want to know. "Are you okay?"

he asked eventually, smoothing a hand down her spine. "You still seem awfully jumpy."

"I'm fine." Gillian dropped her glance self-consciously.

Her shoulders stiff with mounting tension, she moved away from the compelling warmth and intimacy of his touch. She had to get a grip! Her past was not coming back to haunt her!

Deciding it best to concentrate on something that posed no real danger to her, she gathered her supplies and headed briskly for the broken window on the other side of the rustic building.

"Do you think the raccoons'll try and come back in through the office window again?" she asked as she began to sweep up.

"Nope," Cisco said, manning the dustpan while she worked the broom. To her chagrin, he continued to watch her carefully. "It was a fluke they ended up in here in the first place, though after that behemoth storm we had last night you can't blame them for looking for better shelter."

"I guess not," Gillian mused, her embarrassment over the way she had screamed deepening as she located scissors and tape in the desk drawer and dragged a chair to the window, stood on it and stretched plastic over the open window.

"And anyway, it could've been worse," Cisco continued as he stepped up beside her and taped the edges of the plastic in place with long, thick strands of moisture-resistant package-sealing tape. "It could have been a family of skunks in here with us," he said.

Gillian moaned at just the idea. "Don't even joke about that," she admonished, bending slightly to hold the lower edges flat against the frame. Together they finished taping up the window from the inside. Gillian dusted off her hands and stepped back to admire her handiwork. "I guess that will have to do until tomorrow," she said.

"You mean Monday," Cisco corrected.

Very much aware how helpful he had been to her in cleaning up, Gillian slanted him an astonished glance. "We can't get it fixed tomorrow by one of the crew or something?"

"We could get someone to fix it. We just couldn't get the replacement glass." He paused, studying her unease.

Aware he was beginning to read her all too well, Gillian turned her glance away from his probing silver-gray eyes. With his dark hair, ruggedly attractive face, stubborn jaw and sensually chiseled lips, not to mention the expert way he kissed, it would be so easy to let herself be attracted to him. But she couldn't do that. And she knew all the reasons why, even if he didn't.

"Would you feel better if we boarded it up with wood instead?" he asked.

"No. This'll be fine." Gillian picked up the tape and scissors and put them back where she had found them.

"But..." Cisco prodded gently when it was clear she wasn't saying absolutely everything that was on her mind.

"I was just wondering." Gillian's teeth raked across her lower lip as her green eyes lasered into his. Like it or not, she supposed it was time to ask. "Where *are* we going to stay tonight?"

Cisco shrugged. Until now, graced with the mission of helping her, that had been the last thing on his mind. "Your place?" he guessed.

"We can't stay there." Gillian put the broom and dustpan away. "It's only a single room, barely big enough for one person. I'd never sleep a wink."

Like I would with you cuddled beside me? Cisco thought, amused. "Well, the honeymoon cottage Max left us is out, at least for this evening. The road to it was knocked out by the storm last night. Going by past experience, it'll be another twelve or fourteen hours before the water recedes enough for us to get up there. And all the hotels in the area are booked solid with wedding guests."

Gillian's frustration was evident as she removed her apron and hung it up. To his chagrin, she looked as edgy as Cisco felt about the prospect of spending the night together, which in turn made him wonder if she, too, was thinking about the sizzling impact of their earlier kiss.

"Then where?" she asked.

Cisco shrugged, able to think of only one place, as Gillian sat down and exchanged her tennis shoes for satin pumps. He lounged against the wall. "We'll have to stay at my apartment in town, I guess."

"Exactly how many bedrooms does this apartment have?" Gillian asked warily as she undid the knee-high knot in her skirt and let the hem fall back around her ankles.

"One, but there's a pull-out sofa in the living room."

Gillian regarded him silently a long moment. "We don't have any choice here, do we?"

Cisco shrugged. "None that I can think of." Not that it would make much difference where they were, he acknowledged privately. The attraction between them was still going to exist.

"Then I guess it'll have to do," Gillian conceded with a reluctant sigh.

"WHAT DO YOU MEAN Max had all my stuff put in storage?" Gillian asked Tom Turner, the logging camp crew chief, short minutes later.

"He told me you wouldn't be needing it, now that you were going to marry Cisco. Not that there was all that much to begin with," Tom said.

Gillian knew she hadn't brought much with her to Montana. That wasn't the point. "Just tell me where it is, Tom," she insisted, unable to keep the aggravation from her voice.

The burly logging crew chief, who had just recently returned from the wedding celebration himself, stroked his gray-brown beard and shook his head in obvious apology. "I'm afraid I can't do that, Gillian. Max would have my head if I interfered in what he has planned for you and Cisco."

Gillian whirled on Cisco. For the first time in many years, she felt her life was slipping out of her control again in countless ways. "You knew about this?" she demanded.

"Hell, no," Cisco muttered as he raked a hand through his hair and took in the angry expression she leveled on him. "It's the first I've heard of it."

"But it doesn't surprise you?" Gillian ascertained.

Cisco shrugged. "You saw the challenges Max threw out to his other heirs. We'd be fools to think he'd want to test us any less."

"I want my stuff back, Cisco."

"I want you to have your stuff," Cisco stated, looking just as exasperated as she felt.

Gillian whirled back to Tom. "Did Max order you to confiscate Cisco's belongings, too?"

Tom shook his head and planted his work-boot-clad feet even farther apart. "But that doesn't mean he didn't do it," Tom said, crossing his arms squarely in front of him, and giving the newly married couple the once-over. "Just that he didn't order me to do it. Frankly, knowing Max, anything could be happening, even as we speak."

Chapter Four

"Max is not rifling through your stuff, Gillian," Cisco told her dryly as they walked out of her small, dormitory-style room and private bath where she'd been residing. "He did this to throw us for a loop, force us closer together."

Gillian paused to lock the door behind her, though she didn't know why; thanks to Max, there was nothing left there to steal or see. "Well, it isn't working," she declared hotly, pocketing the key and struggling to hide her dismay. What was she going to wear for the next two days or even tonight if she didn't have her own clothes? She couldn't stay in this wedding dress forever, nor could she lounge around clad only in the frilly wedding lingerie! Maybe tomorrow she could cajole her own belongings back from Max or find something else to wear at one of the local clothing stores. But in the meantime, what was she going to do? She certainly couldn't sleep in the buff tonight, not with Cisco under the same roof!

"I beg to differ. It looks like it's working damn

well to me," Cisco drawled, with a humorous shake of his head. Adapting his longer strides to her more dainty ones, he fell in step beside her as they headed for the exit.

She shot him a look as he held the door for her. Unable to resist, he dropped his head to hers. "Don't you feel just a tiny bit closer to me...like we're in this together, come what may?" he asked as she turned sideways and slipped past.

Maybe it would've been nice to fall in love with Cisco, Gillian sighed wistfully, but circumstances demanded a practical husband. One who wouldn't constantly be taking on the role of Sir Galahad, unasked, or kissing her like he meant it. Her head high, Gillian headed for his car. "I don't care if Max's intentions are of the romantic variety. I refuse to be manipulated this way," she announced, as the cool, summery breeze stirred her hair and sent goose bumps over her skin. She refused to fall head over heels in love with Cisco Kidd just because Max McKendrick felt she should!

"Well, whether you intend to get in the spirit of things or not, you may as well get used to unforeseen developments," Cisco said as he stepped forward to hold open the passenger door for her. "At least for the next forty-four hours—"

"Forty-four," Gillian murmured as she glanced at her watch. "Right now that seems like a lifetime to me."

Cisco braced an arm on top of the door as she slid

into the luxuriously appointed bucket seat. "I know what you mean, but maybe there's a way to fix that."

Aware of his hot glance raking over her, Gillian tucked her skirt around her and settled into the smooth leather. "Such as?" Gillian asked stiffly.

"We could both try to have more of a grin-and-bear-it attitude about all this." Cisco flashed her a sexy grin. "'Cause you know what they say." Cisco waited until she had fastened her shoulder belt, before he shut the passenger-side door. "Time flies when you're having fun." He circled lazily around the front of the car.

Gillian watched him slide in beside her and fit the key into the ignition. "You actually don't seem to be minding all that much," she marveled.

"Don't kid yourself," Cisco retorted grimly as the engine sprang to life with an enviable purr. "I have plenty of resentment, too, half of which is directed at myself," he said as he turned to see as he backed out of the parking space in front of the log-cabin-style building.

"Why?" Gillian asked softly as he thrust the sleek car into gear. He was so sure of himself, so sure he could handle everything!

Cisco grimaced and kept his eyes on the road. "For starters, I probably should have seen this coming."

"Because you're his attorney, you mean?" she asked.

"That's part of it. I've worked with Max long enough to know exactly how his mind works—although he can still surprise me from time to time, as he clearly demonstrated tonight. The other part is that Max has treated me like one of the McKendrick family for a long time now." Cisco braked at the approaching intersection, and the beams of the sports car illuminated the lonely two-lane highway between the ranch and town. "Whatever he did for Trace, Patience and Cody, he also did for me." Seeing the coast was clear, Cisco moved his hands confidently on the steering wheel and turned his car onto the smoothly paved road. "I thought I'd be excluded in this particular matchmaking activity because I was instrumental in helping him pull off the other three forty-eight-hour engagements and various 'surprises.'" Cisco frowned, and continued in an introspective voice, rife with exasperation, "I guess I was wrong."

Gillian studied him, and sighed. Though he irritated the heck out of her with his nosiness, Gillian had only to hear the rest of the family talk about Max's young protégé and attorney to know they loved him deeply and considered him to be "family," too. And family was something Gillian did not take for granted. Not since she'd lost her own.

Working hard to express her yearning for close enduring ties, she observed wistfully, "Max loves you like a son, doesn't he?"

Cisco shrugged and kept both hands on the wheel, his emotions held carefully in check. "Yes." Cisco smiled sheepishly after a moment. He shot her an intrigued glance as he adjusted the dials to allow slightly warmer air into the car. "What about you? What is your family going to think about the two of us getting married like this, even if it is only for a couple days?"

Gillian's hand tightened on her purse. She had never wanted to disappoint her parents, and she still didn't. "Thankfully, they'll never have to know about this lunacy—they died in a fire when I was nineteen."

A sorrow-filled silence filled the interior of the car. "I'm sorry." Cisco reached over and lightly squeezed one of the hands in her lap. "You must miss them very much," he said gently.

"Yes, I do," Gillian admitted quietly as unwanted tears sprang to her eyes. She knew the pain she felt over the loss was never going to go away, no matter how many years passed.

A brief silence ensued as they moved from a two-lane highway to a four. Gillian leaned back in her seat and concentrated on the passing scenery. As they got closer to town, the dense woods around the logging camp gradually gave way to gently rolling hills and an occasional country home or small, well-tended ranch.

"Susannah mentioned she met you in a Los Angeles women's shelter ten years ago," Cisco said as they followed the signs toward Fort Benton.

Here it comes again, Gillian thought resentfully. First some sweet talk, and then the gentle but lawyerly third degree. "And you want to know how and why I happened to end up in a shelter, I suppose?'' she surmised with more tartness in her voice than she would have liked. She turned to face him once again.

Cisco sighed and shrugged his broad shoulders noncomittally. ''It crossed my mind.''

Gillian sensed he wasn't going to ease up on her until she told him at least part of her past. Hence, she might as well get it over with. She folded her arms in front of her and began to talk in a clipped, reluctant tone. ''After my parents died, it wasn't a good time for me. Unable to concentrate enough to do my work, I'd dropped out of college. I was scared, drifting, and at that point I had no idea what I wanted to do with my life.'' She shut her eyes at the memory of that miserable time. ''I admit I didn't manage my money very well. And what little money I had went very fast.''

Deliberately she did not recount details of the rest of that year, but slipped on ahead to the time she became involved with Susannah McKendrick.

''I was dead broke when I entered the shelter, and met Susannah, who was one of the volunteers.'' Gratitude filled her heart as she recalled the kindness that had been shown her. ''Susannah told me they were looking for a prep cook in the restaurant she was working in at the time, and she offered to give me a recommendation and help me get hired. From that point on, I worked almost exclusively for and with her.''

"That sounds like Susannah," Cisco replied. "Generous and nurturing to a fault."

Gillian nodded, her affection for her old friend a balm to her lacerated soul. "She's been a very good friend to me."

"As all the McKendricks have been to me," Cisco replied with a similar amount of affection in his voice as they reached the very edge of town.

Eleven o'clock on a Saturday night, the only establishments open were a few gas stations, a twenty-four-hour supermarket and several restaurants. "Why all the questions?" Gillian asked as they passed the square that held the imposing limestone courthouse.

Cisco shrugged as he stopped at a traffic light. "The way I figure it, as long as we're married—even if it is only for a little while, we ought to know a lot more about each other."

Gillian arched her auburn brow at him as they waited for the light to turn green. "I see," she said slowly, anxious to turn the tables on him, too. After all, he wasn't the only one who could ask questions. "Would this include something about your family, too?"

Cisco immediately looked annoyed. "You've met my family—the McKendricks," Cisco reminded her implacably as the light changed and he drove on.

"I meant before that," Gillian insisted as they drove by Pearl's Diner, a homey-looking restaurant with a softly lit interior, large glass windows looking out onto the streets and a handsome Western exterior.

"I know what you meant," Cisco replied, and to her frustration offered nothing further about *his* roots.

"Wait a minute." Cisco hit the brakes as they cruised around the corner, unable to suppress his surprise. "Isn't that Pearl's pickup truck?" He pointed to the sporty pink truck with white leather interior, that sported an extrafancy Pearl's logo on the side.

"Yes," Gillian murmured, still feeling a little piqued he hadn't confided in her, since she'd confided in him. "Why?" she asked Cisco, thinking he could be a most maddening man!

"I thought she'd be with Max tonight," he murmured, obviously perplexed, "especially since the wedding reception is expected to go on 'til long after midnight."

Gillian made a soft dissenting sound. Sometimes men could be so dense! And that went triple for the men from the Silver Spur Ranch!

"I don't know about that," she replied, putting in her two cents and slanting Cisco a wry look as he guided his car into a parking place at the rear of the establishment. "Pearl was still pretty ticked off at Max when we left the wedding reception," Gillian allowed.

"Yeah, I know, but I figured Max would've been able to talk his way out of that by now." Cisco shook his head, perplexed, and continued in a low, subdued tone. "The two of them have been together for as long as I can remember. Although in the past she's been a lot quicker to forgive him." A determined look on his handsome face, Cisco cut the motor and the lights. "I know we're still in our wedding clothes but I want to stop in and make sure everything's okay."

Gillian shrugged and let him know with a glance that whatever he wanted in that regard was fine with her. After all, she was in no hurry to go to his apartment. "It's not like I have anything else to change into," she said dryly.

"True."

Plus, it was June, and brides were literally everywhere. Their unusual attire would probably be overlooked, and if not, so what? "So, you're close to Pearl, too," she noted.

Cisco stepped out of the car and circled around to help Gillian with her door. "Let's just say she was a mom and a friend and a big sister all rolled into one, when I needed her," he confided as he flattened a hand over Gillian's spine and escorted her around to the entrance. "I owe her a lot. Besides, if she is in the diner, maybe Max'll be there, too." Cisco grinned mischieviously. "And we can both give him a piece of our mind for the way he had all your belongings packed up and spirited away."

"Sounds good to me," Gillian said as she squared her slender shoulders resolutely. "I want that stuff back!"

PEARL WAS BEHIND the long wooden bar that served those who came in intending to eat alone. She had changed out of the clothes she'd worn to the wedding, into her pink waitress uniform, white apron and white Western boots. Her bright red hair was, as usual, pinned into a high French twist, but this time there were tendrils escaping to softly frame her face and the back of her neck. And that was unusual, Cisco thought. Pearl always coated her hair with enough hairspray to hold it in place in even the stiffest Montana wind.

"Hey, Pearl, thought you'd still be at the reception," Cisco began casually, hoping he could work some of the matchmaking magic his mentor now seemed to possess in spades.

"You two ducked out early, too," Pearl remarked, ushering the two of them to a cozy wooden booth by the window. She gave Cisco a measuring look. "And I didn't see either of you eat any dinner."

Cisco grinned at Pearl's unabashed attempt to mother him and Gillian, but made no move to resist it. "That's 'cause we didn't," he answered cheerfully.

"Then the two of you sit right down and I'll get you whatever you want, on the house." Her manner brisk and businesslike, Pearl handed them both menus and whipped out her order pad as they slid across the padded leather seats. "Tonight's special is country-fried steak, drowning in cream gravy, with whipped potatoes and collard greens."

"The special sounds great," Gillian said.

"To me, too," Cisco added.

With her slender shoulders stiff with tension, undoubtedly lingering from her fight with Max at the reception, Pearl scrawled down their order, then looked up again. Her pretend-there's-nothing-wrong expression spoke volumes. "Can I get you two a couple of green salads to go with that?"

"Sure," Cisco said, intentionally ignoring the unmistakable tinge of sadness in Pearl's eyes. "I'll have ranch dressing on mine."

"Sounds great," Gillian agreed. She exchanged concerned looks with Cisco, before turning back to Pearl. "I'll have the ranch, too."

"I'll bring it right out." Pearl went back into the kitchen. Short minutes later, she came out of the swinging double doors, two crisp green salads in hand. She set them in front of Gillian and Cisco, along with a basket of hot rolls and butter. Knowing it was now or never, Cisco reached out and caught Pearl's hand before she could get away. "Sit with us a minute, Pearl," he urged, knowing the high-backed booth would allow them a measure of privacy.

Gillian scooted over and made room for Pearl as she added softly, "We can see you're upset."

"As anyone would be, after what Max put you through," Cisco added.

"I'm not complaining." Pearl took a seat at the end of the booth, beside Gillian. "What Max did brought me to my senses," she confided with weary sadness. "It made me face some things I should've confronted a mighty long time ago."

"Like what?" Cisco asked, as he forked up some greens.

Pearl sighed. "Like the fact that maybe I *am* the marrying kind after all." Pearl took a lace-edged hankie out of her bodice and dabbed at the fresh tears sparkling in her eyes. She swallowed hard and it was a moment before she could go on. "I don't know. Maybe it was something about seeing Trace and Susannah, Patience and Josh, and Cody and Callie together again, but as I watched them all pledge their undying love for each other and speak their vows, I realized I don't want to spend the rest of my life as a single woman."

"How long have you and Max known each other?" Gillian asked, taking a sip of her water.

"We've been close for twenty-five years now," Pearl admitted, twisting her capable hands together. "Enough to have a silver wedding anniversary. Instead, all I have to show for it is this diner, of which I admit I've made a grand success, and more expensive presents than I can shake a stick at!"

"You still love Max, then?" Gillian persisted, while Cisco listened intently.

"It doesn't matter what I feel." Pearl stood abruptly. She crumpled her hankie and tucked it back into the bodice of her uniform, then smoothed the clinging fabric over her hips.

"Now, Pearl, I know Max loves you with all his heart and soul," Cisco protested, before his friend could run away.

"Oh, really." Pearl slapped both hands on hips that were as slender as a teenage girl's. "Then why—if he believes in marriage so much for his kin, and even you and Gillian, Cisco—didn't he lasso the two of us together for forty-eight hours and then end that with a marriage proposal and a wedding ring?'' she demanded belligerently.

Cisco spread his hands wide. ''I don't know, Pearl. Maybe he didn't want to mess things up by changing them. Maybe he thought you liked things the way they were, too.''

Pearl leaned forward abruptly and slammed the table with her fist. ''Darn it all, Cisco. Stop defending that bounder and just admit he isn't committed to me.''

''Now, Pearl—'' Cisco began cautiously. He had the sinking feeling, despite his best intentions, that he'd just made things worse.

''Don't you 'Now Pearl' me, Cisco Kidd!'' Pearl fumed. ''You tell that old rapscallion this! You tell him I never want to see him again, and to put that in his pipe and smoke it!'' Pearl stomped off. The doors to the kitchen swung shut behind her.

Gillian and Cisco finished their salads in silence as Cisco tried vainly to figure out how to repair the situation. And he was still thinking on it when another waitress cleared their salad plates and brought out two plates of fragrant, steaming food and a complimentary basket of warm and flaky buttermilk biscuits.

''This is really upsetting you, isn't it?'' Gillian asked as she spread butter and homemade peach jelly on her biscuit.

"I've never known them to be anything but to-gether. To this point, I've never really even seen them fight," Cisco admitted as he cut into his steak.

"Maybe they'll make up pretty quickly."

Cisco shook his head. He didn't have any illusions on that score. Gillian shouldn't, either. "I have a feel-ing that is not going to happen unless Max proposes."

Gillian brought a forkful of fluffy mashed potatoes to her lips. "You don't think he will?"

Cisco shrugged. Aware his appetite had faded, he continued to eat nonetheless. "Up to this point, Pearl and Max had agreed they weren't the marrying kind."

"Only now she's changed her mind," Gillian sur-mised, as she swiftly cleaned her plate, finished off her biscuit and buttered and jellied another.

"Right." Cisco nodded. "And as far as I know, Max hasn't."

Another silence fell as the waitress returned and left them with a pitcher of cream and a carafe of hot coffee. "I guess I could play matchmaker," Cisco said eventually, as he poured the rich brew for both himself and Gillian—who surprised him by downing yet a third biscuit.

"But you don't really want to, do you?" Gillian asked, stirring generous amounts of both cream and sugar into her coffee.

"I've always accepted advice from Max—not the other way around—at least when it comes to personal matters. Legal matters are different, since I'm his attorney now. Though even on that score, I've learned a lot from Max, too.''

Gillian studied Cisco. "You don't think he'd listen to you if you tried to intervene in this situation with him and Pearl?" Gillian asked.

Cisco sighed. "I'm not sure he'd listen to anyone on this. And why should he? It's his love life.''

"It's our love life, too," Gillian said after they'd paid the bill and headed back outside. She was glad to have something—and someone—else to focus on beside her own situation with Cisco. "That hasn't stopped Max from interfering," she added as Cisco helped her into the car.

"That's different." Cisco climbed in beside her.

"How so?" Gillian queried as he started the car and drove several streets south.

Cisco parked in front of a building that looked very much like a stable from the Old West. He cut the motor and briefly rested his broad shoulders against the back of his seat. An affectionate note crept into his low, commiserating tone. "Max is just trying to set his affairs in order and make sure his property goes to the people he wants to have it, while he's still around to see to it that things are done right.''

Gillian blinked as the next thought hit. "He's not sick or anything, is he?" Gillian asked worriedly as Cisco came around to hold her door for her.

"Heck no," Cisco replied, one warm hand closing protectively on her waist as he helped her out. "Max is as healthy as a horse. But he is also—in his own words—'as old as the hills now.' Which could be the real reason why he doesn't want to marry Pearl," Cisco continued, bringing her closer yet. "Max has a good twenty years on Pearl, I'd guess." Cisco paused to locate the door key. "He's probably worried he'd become ill at some point and she'll have to spend the rest of her life nursing him."

Gillian sighed as she leaned against the wooden building that was painted a very dark brown. "Well, right now it's not their age keeping them apart, but Max's insensitivity to Pearl's feelings," she said, as Cisco began to unlock the heavy oak-and-brass door.

Cisco stopped in midmotion and turned to her with a knowing smirk. "Uh-oh."

"What?" Gillian replied, welcoming the opportunity to match wits with him.

"Here it comes. The part where you lambaste all men," Cisco drawled, stepping back and holding up both hands in a facetious parody of surrender.

Gillian couldn't help it; she grinned. This was a side of Cisco she hadn't seen—and liked. "If the chaps and spurs fit," she quipped with exaggerated seriousness.

Cisco narrowed his eyes in mock censure. "Hey—" he arrowed a thumb at his chest and sparred right back "—all men are *not* insensitive jerks."

"Right." Gillian nodded with playful amiability. "Some are *sensitive* jerks."

Cisco moved, so she was trapped against the side

of the building, just right of the front door. "I resent that," he told her with an amused twinkle in his eyes.

"I'm sure you do," Gillian replied, a giggle escaping from her lips.

Grinning, Cisco placed a hand against the wall next to her head and leaned in close. "On behalf of all men everywhere, I demand a retraction," he teased.

Gillian grinned back, aware, but not surprised, at the way her heart was racing at his nearness. She'd known, when she kissed him back at the wedding, there were considerable sparks between them. That didn't mean she should surrender to those sparks, however. Especially when she knew this spur-of-the-moment marriage of theirs was soon going to end.

Forcing herself to ignore the excitement racing through her, the sensual tingle in her arms and legs, Gillian slipped beneath his outstretched arm and replied, "Oh, you do, do you?"

"Yep," he said, not dropping his eyes from hers.

"I'll give it some thought," Gillian drawled, reminding herself firmly she had secrets she still needed to keep. That would not be done if she allowed him to get too close to her. She regarded him cheerfully. Took a deep, bracing breath. "Now, are you going to show me this building of yours, or not?"

"You look surprised," Cisco said as they walked inside and he switched on the lights. He showed her through the first floor with the elegantly appointed reception area, adjacent private law library, secretary's office and private office. Upstairs, on the second floor, he took her through the combination kitchen and living area, the bathroom and single bedroom.

"It's so...tidy." She stepped across the polished wood floor and peered into the walk-in closet. Her eyes scanned the row of freshly dry-cleaned business suits, starched shirts and handcrafted leather boots. "There doesn't appear to be a single item out of place," she continued, impressed, as she stepped away from the closet and toward the big brass-framed bed.

Cisco had a firm policy of only taking credit where it was due. "I have a maid service that comes in once a week to do the cleaning." Cisco guided her back into the living area with the saddle-brown leather sofa bed and custom-made wagon-wheel coffee table before heading back into the kitchen. Cisco watched her peruse the stove, microwave and indoor grill—none of which he'd put to use—but the delight in her eyes faded as she peered into the refrigerator.

"Cisco, there's nothing in here but beer, coffee and orange juice!"

He shrugged. As far as he was concerned, that was all he needed. "I eat out almost all the time—with clients at fancy restaurants and with Max at Pearl's."

"You don't cook at all, then?"

"Not unless you consider beverages cooking."

"No, I don't." She shook her head at him and gave

him a vaguely pitying look. "You really need to learn."

Cisco didn't know why. He didn't have anyone to cook for. He sauntered closer. "You going to teach me?"

As he'd expected she would, she stepped away. "Maybe. If we have nothing else to do."

Cisco could think of plenty of things he'd rather do with Gillian than slave over a hot stove. But none of those things would help him find out what was troubling her.

"Besides," Gillian continued, albeit a little nervously now that he'd tried to get close to her again, "it takes a lot more than just spending a couple of days and nights together under one roof or embarking on shared activities to make a marriage."

I agree. It takes trust. And that was something they didn't have and wouldn't be likely to gain when both were so wiped out. Cisco paused. "Are you as beat as I am?" Maybe everything—including their spur-of-the-moment marriage—would seem easier in the morning.

Gillian nodded. "It's been a long day."

"For me, too," Cisco admitted with relief.

"If you don't mind calling it a night," Gillian said, looking consoled by the idea of a long, nocturnal time-out from the intimacy of spending time with each other, "then I for one would be glad to go our separate ways until morning."

"Not at all." Glad they were in synch about this,

Cisco went into the bedroom and returned carrying two pillows, a stack of linens and a blanket. "Though I doubt separate beds are what Max had in mind for us," he continued as he set the linens down on the end table next to the sofa bed.

"In some instances," Gillian said defiantly, putting her purse carefully down on the kitchen counter, "we know best."

Cisco took off the sofa cushions and neatly set them out of the way. He sized her up and decided a little time and space were what she needed. "I'll sleep out here," he said matter-of-factly.

Gillian immediately disagreed as she swept over to assist him. "I don't want to put you out of your own bed."

Cisco straightened and regarded her in a gentlemanly manner. He wanted her to have her privacy, though he wasn't sure he was too excited about the prospect of having her sleep in his bed, either. Forever after he'd likely be haunted by hotly envisioned images of her between his sheets, and the lingering floral scent of her on his pillows.

"You should have the bedroom," he repeated, even more firmly.

Gillian folded her arms in front of her and continued to look mutinous. To Cisco's chagrin, she seemed to be thinking about the downside of sleeping in his bed, too. "I'd rather have the sofa bed," she said just as stubbornly.

It wasn't worth arguing about. "Fine." In one

swift, smooth motion Cisco pulled the mattress out by the metal handle and unfolded it. "I'll help you make it up."

"That's not necessary." Gillian stepped between Cisco and the bed. "I can do it." She took the stack of linens and held them to her chest like a protective shield.

Cisco paused, not certain he liked the feeling of being treated as a lustful schoolboy in search of a female to bed, even if that was the direction of his forbidden thoughts and fantasies. "You're sure?" he asked casually.

She nodded.

"All right, then." Giving up on the gentlemanly thing to do, he turned to leave, wondering how he was even going to feign sleep when every inch of him was on fire with desire.

"Cisco?"

Her gentle voice stopped him dead in his tracks. Pulse racing, he turned back. A flush of color pinkened her cheeks. "I hate to ask, but since I have no clothes of my own at the moment, save what I'm wearing, and I can't very well sleep in a wedding dress..." She gestured inanely and her voice trailed off.

"You want to borrow something to sleep in?" he guessed.

She searched his eyes, looking for the slightest sign he was put out. "Would you mind?" she asked hesitantly, still looking embarrassed at having to ask.

"No. Not at all," Cisco fibbed. Now, along with the memories of her in his apartment, he thought wistfully, he'd have the memories of her in his pajamas. 'Course, staying here still had to be better than staying in the honeymoon cottage. This had to be a lot less romantic setting.

He slipped into the bedroom and came back with a pair of flannel pajamas. Gillian looked at the pattern of cowboys and lassos and horses and broke out into a smile. "They were a gag gift, years ago," he explained tersely, not wanting her to think he had picked them out for himself.

Gillian's eyes sparkled with lively curiosity. "From Max?"

"Patience," Cisco corrected. "I wore them a couple of times at Max's place when I had a heck of a case of the flu, and the McKendricks were nursing me through the worst of it."

"But you haven't worn them since," she said, remarking on the fact they were soft and thick and practically like new.

"No. Patience laundered them and sent them home with me. I put them in a drawer and haven't needed them 'til now."

Gillian shook her head. "After hearing the story behind these pajamas I'm not so sure I should sleep in them," she teased.

"Well, you're going to have to if you want to wear pajamas," Cisco quipped dryly. He spread his hands wide. "It's the only pair I've got."

That threw her for a loop, but she recovered quickly enough. "What do you normally sleep in?" she asked after a moment.

"The buff."

Gillian rolled her eyes in obvious exasperation. "Well, that won't do," she scolded sternly. "As long as we're under one roof, I *insist* we both wear nightclothes of some sort."

"How come?" he taunted, sauntering even nearer.

Gillian backed up until the backs of her knees touched the sofa-bed mattress. "Trust me on this, Cisco," she said as twin spots of color swept into her cheeks. "We need to stick to some level of propriety."

"Even if it's our wedding night?" he drawled.

"Especially because it's our wedding night," she returned. "Therefore, I'll take the pajama top." Demonstrating, she held it against her slender form for size. "It comes down to midthigh anyway, which is almost as long as a nightshirt. And you can wear the bottoms, Cisco."

Cisco knew she was trying to lessen the erotic tension between them. He wasn't sure this was the way to go. The thought of her in nothing but that shirt caused a heat wave as big as all Montana in his lower half.

"Promise me, Cisco. You'll wear half if I wear half."

"Fine." Cisco swallowed around the sudden parched feeling in his throat and the throbbing in his groin. "I promise." If splitting one pair of pajamas between them made her feel better, more protected in a sexual sense, so be it. However, judging by the hardening state of his lower half, her proposal was having the opposite effect on him. Figuring he better get out of there before she noticed the burgeoning change in his anatomy he said, "If you don't need anything else..."

She smiled briskly and avoided his eyes. "Just your shower."

He pointed to the green and black tiled room situated to the left of both the bedroom and living area. "Help yourself. You should find everything you need in there. I've even got a new toothbrush in the drawer, so have it."

"Thanks," Gillian said, already heading quickly toward the bathroom, his pajama top clasped in her arms. "I'll see you in the morning."

Cisco nodded thoughtfully, knowing even if she didn't what a long, sleepless night this was likely to be, at least for him. "You, too."

GILLIAN EMERGED FROM the bathroom and climbed into bed, exhausted, but wired. It had been one incredible twenty-four hours. The storm last night followed by a full day putting together emergency provisions at the dining hall. Then the McKendrick wedding, Max's surprise appearance, followed by more celebrating and Max's daring suggestion that she and Cisco marry.

She'd agreed because she was tired of running and because the questions Cisco had been pestering her with proved to her beyond a shadow of a doubt that she needed a new identity that was both legal and rock solid.

She'd figured if she had all that, plus the protection of the McKendrick wealth and name, she would finally be able to stop looking over her shoulder and worrying her past would catch up with her, and begin to live again.

What she hadn't counted on was Cisco. How safe he'd make her feel, and at the same time how threatened. If she spent too much time with him, she had the sinking feeling she could very well lose her heart to this man.

But nearly six hours of marriage had already passed. What were another forty-two, really, she told herself confidently, when so very much was at stake? She just had to get through another couple days of this marriage and then she'd be safe again. Protected. Married or not, she'd have a "family" in the McKendricks and a place where she belonged, and the vast dining hall business on the ranch would be hers.

For the first time in her life, she would be able to experiment with recipes to her heart's content and run her kitchen exactly the way she wanted to run it, with no interference from anyone.

As far as Cisco went…well, she knew she could deal with him. She just had to be careful not to let herself get too caught up in this ridiculous matchmaking scheme of Max's. And she could do that, too, she thought, as she opened the secret compartment she'd had built into the bottom of her purse, retrieved what she needed and climbed back into bed.

JUST AFTER MIDNIGHT, Cisco lay on his back in the dark, hands folded behind his head, as an hour passed. Then another. And another. Normally not one to have trouble sleeping, he was frustrated but not surprised by his inability to sleep.

Sighing, Cisco finally threw back the covers and got up. Maybe if he had a cold beer he'd be able to fall asleep. Certainly, it would help him to relax and stop thinking hopelessly protective and erotic thoughts about his new bride in the next room. Because if there was one thing that was not going to happen tonight—regardless of the wily Max's hopes to the contrary—it was any sort of a honeymoon. He and Gillian had both agreed wholeheartedly on that.

Pretty sure Gillian had fallen asleep a long time ago, he soundlessly eased open the bedroom door. Sure enough, she was breathing deep and even. And curled on her side, the covers drawn up to her chest. Her long auburn curls were tousled like a halo of crumpled silk around her head, her lips soft and bare and slightly parted, her cheeks flushed pink against the fairness of her skin. Where her flannel top gaped open, midsternum, he could see the uppermost curve of her breasts, and the even sexier hollow in between.

Suppressing a groan of renewed desire, Cisco

turned his glance away. Determined not to disturb her in the slightest, he moved barefoot across the room and headed for the kitchen.

And it was at that moment, as he edged quietly past her that she woke with a startled gasp, reached under her pillow and presented him with an even bigger surprise.

Chapter Five

"What in the heck..." Cisco whispered, stunned, as he found himself looking down the barrel of a very small but very deadly gun.

"I told you what would happen if you came back," Gillian said, in a voice thick with both confusion and sleep. "I told you I wouldn't let you terrorize me again." She gripped the barrel with hands that shook and stared at him with eyes that were wide with fright.

"Terrorize you how?" Cisco demanded. To his frustration, she didn't answer, didn't move. "What have I done, Gillian?" Cisco asked, even more firmly.

"You know very well what you've done...." she said, her voice rising angrily as she continued to aim the gun straight at his chest.

His jaw tensing, for he knew there was no way he could survive a bullet wound at such close range, Cisco stayed where he was and lifted his hands in surrender. "Put the gun down, Gillian, and we'll talk," he ordered.

But she didn't seem to see him at all. "Never

again," she murmured thickly instead, as tears streamed down her face. "I told you...this was never going to happen again...and I meant it, Phillip," she whispered hoarsely. "I meant it with every fiber of my being."

Phillip! Who was Phillip? And why did she think he was Phillip? Was she dreaming? In the midst of some terrible nightmare? Not that this explained her sleeping with a gun under her pillow, for Pete's sake! A gun she had to have carried with her on her person or in her purse. Both options were damned unsettling, to say the least. She was obviously in far more trouble than she'd let on. No wonder she didn't want anyone asking questions or looking into her past.

"Gillian, listen to me," he began patiently, imbuing his voice with as much tranquillity and kindness as possible, as his heart thudded all the harder. "It's Cisco—"

Again she appeared not to hear him. "You have no right to be here," Gillian said. Her lips tightened determinedly as she released the safety.

Talk about nightmares! "Put the gun down, Gillian."

Still deep in her dream, she lifted the gun slightly, the whole of her trembling. "I'm warning you. Don't come any closer! I'll shoot!" The barrel of the gun jerked up as she put one hand up as if to ward off a blow. "I promise you I will!" she stated again. Then the gun came down once more, and locked into shooting position. Her left hand closed over her right in steadying fashion.

Cisco knew time had run out. He wasn't going to let her hurt herself or him. In one smooth motion, he ducked and dove for the sofa bed. His body covered hers and he knocked her body flat, her hands up above her head just as the gun went off with a resounding...*click?*

It wasn't loaded, Cisco thought, as relief swept over him in a staggering wave. Or at least not all the way, Cisco decided as he struggled to get the gun away from her and Gillian began to scream. Given no other choice, he forced the gun from her hand and cut off her shriek with a hand clamped tight across her mouth. "You're dreaming, Gillian," Cisco said, giving her a little shake. "Do you hear me? You're dreaming, Gillian. And there's no reason to be afraid. You're here with me. Cisco. In my apartment. No one is going to hurt you. Do you hear me, Gillian? No one is going to hurt you."

Abruptly his staunchly uttered words penetrated. She stopped struggling. Tears still streaming down her face, she gazed up at him in a combination of horror and relief that let him know she was fully awake, if confused as hell as to what was now going on with the two of them.

Sorry he'd had to be so rough with her, Cisco eased his hand from her mouth. Saw her lower lip tremble all the more and tried not to notice that the pajama top she wore was twisted up around her waist, revealing long satin-smooth legs, a slender waist and gently curving hips, clad in transparent white lace panties.

"What happened?" she asked shakily, pulling the flannel pajama top down to midthigh.

Good question, Cisco thought as he rolled away from her and sat up. What the hell had happened? "I couldn't sleep and came out, intending to get a cold beer out of the refrigerator. Before I got all the way to the kitchen, you sat up and pulled a gun on me. I assume you were dreaming."

Gillian released a tremulous sigh and raked trembling hands through the tousled layers of her auburn hair. "I was," she said shakily.

Cisco sat down on the sofa-bed mattress, still warm from her body heat. "Does this happen often? The nightmares," he added when she continued to look vulnerable and confused.

"Only when I'm overtired or upset." She shivered again and drew her knees up to her chest. "I'm sorry." She closed her eyes in abject misery and rested the side of her face against her upraised knees. She still seemed to be struggling to get a hold of herself. "I never should have held a gun on you."

She was right about that, Cisco thought. He did not like surprises of any kind, never mind ones so potentially deadly. He also sensed there was a damn good reason for everything Gillian did, thought or said. His need to take care of her increased tenfold.

"Do you always sleep with a gun under your pillow?" He began his information gathering casually, wondering once again who or what she was running from, and if her experiences had been anywhere near as devastatingly lonely or physically brutal as his own.

Gillian lifted her head and looked him in the eye. Vulnerable or not, she was not about to be taken advantage of. "I have for a long while," she said in a way that just dared him to make something of it.

Cisco took her hand in his and lifted it to his lips. Ignoring the subtle tensing of her arm beneath his questing touch, he lightly traced the silky underside of her wrist with his fingertips. "Why?" he asked gently. Was she on the lam, or just in danger of some kind?

Her chin took on the stubborn tilt he was beginning to know all too well. Gillian withdrew her hand from his and aimed a killer look at him. "Look, I'm sorry for what I did just now, but why I do what I do is really none of your business."

Cisco's patience began to fade as she turned her glance to the moonlight streaming in through the open second-floor windows. "My wife's problems are mine," he told her firmly.

Gillian tossed her head. Her silky auburn curls fell over her shoulder every which way. "Maybe that'd be the case if we were married in more than name only," Gillian began uncertainly as color swept into her high, delicately sculpted cheeks.

Aware she looked even more beautiful now than

she had in her wedding dress, Cisco struggled to keep his desire for her in check. "It's the case whether we ever sleep together or not," Cisco said, realizing it was true. Wise or not, he cared what happened to her—now, and in the past—to make her behave this way. And this surprised him. Gillian did not seem like a good bet to stick around, and that fact alone ought to have had him running in the opposite direction. Yet he was drawn to her, more drawn to her than he had ever been to any woman. Furthermore, now that he knew she was in more trouble than even he had dreamed, he wanted to protect her. But to protect her he first had to get her to trust him and confide in him. "Does it have anything to do with Phillip?" he asked softly.

"What do you know about Phillip?" she asked suspiciously, drawing the covers up around her waist.

Cisco leaned very close to her. "Just that you wanted to shoot him. Or tried to just now," he explained in a quiet tone, wishing she would make it easier for him to comfort her.

"Yes, well, had the man in my nightmare been here, which he clearly wasn't, except in my dream, he would've deserved it," she said bitterly.

"Because he terrorized you or threatened you somehow?" Cisco probed, remembering what she had said in her sleep.

"I think I'll have a cold beer, too," Gillian said, changing the subject nervously. She threw off the covers, lowered her spectacular legs and padded toward the kitchen, her hips moving with subtle, albeit unconscious, sexiness beneath the hem of the pajama top. "Want to join me?"

Trying not to notice her soft enticing curves, Cisco followed her to the refrigerator. "Sure."

She removed two bottles from the refrigerator and closed the door. Their hands brushed and their eyes met as she handed the beer to him. He twisted off the cap by hand while she used the bottle opener on the counter. Wordlessly, she plunked the metal cap into the trash, returned to the sofa bed and settled languidly in the corner.

Cisco watched Gillian draw the covers up around her waist once again and knew she considered the conversation about her nightmare over. As far as he was concerned, they were just getting started.

Obviously, Gillian perceived herself to be in some kind of danger. If he was going to help her, and he was determined to help her, he had to find out more about why this Phillip would want to hurt her. He had to know what he was up against if he was going to give her her future back and at the same time protect everyone else on the ranch from getting caught up in the violence of Gillian's past, too. "Gillian..."

She lifted her gaze to his. Gave an officious smile. "I know you are trying to be gallant in the Old West way and come to the aid of a lady, as any good gentleman would do," she said stubbornly. "But I really think, in this case, the less you know the better."

Cisco sat down beside her, on the edge of the sofa

bed. He took a sip of his beer and watched her gaze drop to his bare chest and the way his nipples were contracting in the pleasantly cool night air. "I know where you're coming from, Gillian. It's never been easy for me to accept help, either."

She sipped her beer and wiped the moisture from her lips with the back of her hand. "Really."

Ignoring her droll tone, Cisco continued, "I haven't always been an angel, either."

Gillian turned her dazzling green eyes heavenward, as determined, it seemed, to keep their conversation on a superficial note as he was to deepen it. "Although, like everyone else on the ranch, I've heard the rumors about your supposedly nefarious past, I still find them very hard to believe," she said, running a hand through the length of her auburn hair, shifting it off her face.

"Believe it," Cisco said gruffly. The truth was he was still pretty embarrassed and ashamed about some of the things he had done as a kid, but he had managed to put it all behind him, and so could Gillian.

Cisco caught her hand before it fell back into her lap. Ignoring her mutinous expression, he confided, determined to get her to depend on him a little bit whether she wanted to or not, "When Max and I first met, I didn't want Max's help any more than you want mine, Gillian, but Max gave it to me anyway. I tried everything I knew to make him give up on me and go away, the way everyone else had, but he wouldn't do it. He said he saw something worthwhile in me that he wasn't going to waste.''

Gillian stiffened and removed her hand from his. She took another drink. ''Thanks ever so much for the charming parable, Cisco,'' she said with lethal contentiousness that upped the tension between them another notch, ''but I don't need saving.''

Don't you? Cisco thought as he shook his head at her remonstratively. ''That gun you've been snuggling up to at night says otherwise.''

Flushing, Gillian drained the rest of her beer in one long thirsty gulp and set the empty bottle aside with a thud. ''Look, I'm sorry I mistook you for the burglar of my dreams.'' She defended herself hotly. ''But the gun wasn't loaded. It never is. I just keep it with me for protection, in case anything does happen.''

Cisco studied the flushed contours of her angel's face. ''And it has happened in the past, hasn't it?'' he queried as he put his empty bottle next to hers.

''I've had nightmares before,'' Gillian replied, choosing—he thought—to deliberately misunderstand his question. ''Everyone has.''

Cisco lifted a disbelieving brow as he shot a look at the gun on the table. ''The kind of nightmare that prompts you to mistake an innocent bystander for someone named Phillip and try to shoot him?'' he mocked dryly. ''I don't think so.''

Gillian's green eyes grew stormy, even as Cisco savored the moonlit darkness and the intimacy of being together like this on such a quiet summer night.

"I'm sorry I did that," she said. "And for your information, that's never happened to me before." The flush in her cheeks deepened and she began to trace patterns on the blanket with soft, aimless strokes of her fingertips. "It's just that I'm not used to having a man in my quarters with me when I sleep and you woke me in the middle of a bad dream. And when I saw your silhouette moving toward me, looking so dark and dangerous...I thought my dream was real."

She looked upset about that, as she should be, Cisco thought. He tore his glance from the caressing motions of her hand. "Which brings us back to the original question," Cisco said, forcing them to get back to the heart of the matter. "Who is Phillip and what did Phillip do to you?" Cisco asked more aggressively. If it was half as bad as Cisco thought, he wanted to pulverize the barbarian.

Gillian's hand stilled. "You're not going to give up on this, are you?"

Cisco surveyed the tense set of her slender shoulders. "Nope."

Gillian released a resigned breath and after another long pause, appeared to come to some kind of decision. Swallowing hard, she looked up at him, the pain and devastation of what had happened reflected in her eyes. "A long time ago, right before I met Susannah, I was stalked and my apartment was broken into a couple of times, mostly when I wasn't there—to terrorize me, I guess—but once I was there when the break-in occurred."

"What happened?"

Gillian shrugged and didn't meet his eyes. As each moment passed, she seemed to withdraw into herself a little more. "I called the police, of course, but they let the guy go."

This, Cisco did not understand. "Why?" he asked, his own frustration evident.

Sighing heavily, Gillian raked her hands through her hair again and looked all the more distressed. "Because I knew him and had had a relationship with him and there wasn't enough evidence to arrest him."

"But if he'd broken in, surely there was proof."

"He had a background in intelligence work before I met him. There was no lock, no alarm system he couldn't get around. He was also a number of years older than I was at the time, and as far as the police were concerned, because I was so completely hysterical about everything, he had a lot more credibility. Anyway—" Gillian sighed shakily "—rather than continue to deal with it, or try to prove to the police that he was the one who was lying and not me, I walked out on my lease and used every cent I had to get as far away as I could from him."

"Which is how you ended up in a homeless shelter in California," Cisco guessed.

"Right." Giving him no chance to ask questions about her time in the shelter, she rushed on. "Once there, I put my life back together pretty quickly again, but ever since, as you can probably understand, I've been a little leery. So, to help feel safe again, I took lessons at a shooting range and bought a gun.''

Gillian bit her lower lip and shook her head, continuing, ''I tried sleeping with it loaded and nearby, but I was always afraid it was going to go off accidentally. So I stopped carrying it loaded and contented myself with knowing I had a few bullets to put in the gun, and that even unloaded, it would work effectively to scare off an intruder, although that doesn't seem to be the case here. Does it?''

Cisco recalled how he'd felt when confronted with her weapon. ''Don't bet on that. You scared the heck out of me.''

''But you got the gun away from me anyway. Which means anyone else could've, too,'' Gillian pointed out, troubled.

Cisco studied her, then finally guessed unhappily, ''Which means you're still frightened of being accosted.''

Gillian shrugged and replied, ''In and of itself, that is not surprising. Once you realize your vulnerabilities, the apprehension doesn't really go away. Although it is better for me now. Or has been, since I learned how to shoot and started carrying a gun.''

''On your person, or in your purse?'' Cisco inquired matter-of-factly. Although he was pleased Gillian had confided in him as much as she had, his gut instinct told him Gillian was still concealing a lot.

''In my purse, most of the time. Occasionally, on my person—if I have to be out alone late at night.''

"This was in Los Angeles," Cisco ascertained, wondering what else she was holding back.

"Yes," she bit out.

Cisco could almost understand that. In recent years, cities like Los Angeles had become hotbeds of crime and violence. But they weren't in the big city. "Here, in Montana, have you felt the need to do the same?" he asked gently.

"No. At least not so far. I've felt very safe on the Silver Spur Ranch, very protected," Gillian admitted in a soft voice. "It's one of the reasons I was willing to go through this forty-eight-hour charade so I could run the food business and stay here permanently."

Cisco paused, pleased to see her instincts were on target in this regard. "You're right to think the men and women here would lay down their lives to protect each other. We're like family. It's one of the reasons I like it here, too. But as for you carrying a gun, Gillian, you shouldn't have to resort to that to feel safe, no matter where you live. No one should."

Gillian shifted restlessly. She drew her knees up to her chest, beneath the covers, and rested her chin on her knees. If she were really his wife, in something more than name only, maybe she would believe that. "Easier said than done, believe me," she muttered.

"Maybe it is," Cisco told her gently, his heart going out to her.

Gillian lifted her head, for one brief moment looking as though she wanted to take shelter in his arms, every bit as much as he wanted to offer it. "And how is that?" she challenged, just as softly.

Cisco knew it was not going to be easy for Gillian to learn to trust any man again, but more than anything he wanted to make the uneasiness in her eyes go away. And that process was going to involve risk on both their parts.

"I think I could make you feel safe." *If you'd let me.*

She looked taken aback by his proposal. "Really. How?" she asked, skeptical.

The easiest way in the world, Cisco thought as his entire being warmed to the task. "By watching over you," he said.

"Watching over me or watching me?" Gillian asked as her heart took on a slow, thudding beat.

Cisco gave her a sexy grin that turned her whole world upside down. "I could see myself doing both."

"And how exactly are you going to do that?" Gillian drawled, knowing deliciously dangerous complications like this were exactly what she had been trying to avoid all these years. She didn't want to drag anyone else into the nightmare of fear and uncertainty that had become her life. She didn't want to tear down the barricades she had erected around her heart. But that was, it appeared, exactly what Cisco Kidd was trying to do.

"It would depend on what time of day or night it was," he said with a teasing wink.

Gillian glanced at her watch. "All right. I'll play

along,'' she said dryly, her gut feeling telling her that Cisco would not rest until he'd had a chance to prove his point. ''What would you do at three-thirty in the morning to make me feel safe, Cisco?'' For that matter, what could anyone do to make her nightmares go away?

''This is after a bad dream.''

''Right,'' Gillian said, aware her heart was pounding in her throat again and he was very, very close. Close enough for her to inhale the intoxicating scent of his skin and cologne.

''Well, first, I'd climb into bed beside you—if I wasn't already there—and I'd take you in my arms,'' he said softly. Ignoring her wide-eyed amazement, he lifted the covers, slid in beside her, so they were situated shoulder to shoulder in the warmth.

''Then I'd hold you close,'' he continued, wrapping one strong arm around her protectively and cuddling her close. ''Just like this.'' He threaded his other hand through the hair at the nape of her neck and angling her head beneath his, pressed a kiss to the top of her head. Another on her temple. Her cheek. ''And I'd hold you like this until you stopped trembling.''

Gillian's face rested against the beard-roughened warmth of his. Had it ever felt so good to simply be held? she wondered wistfully as she snuggled against the rock-solid heat of his chest. Had she ever felt so safe, so protected, so absolutely and tenderly cared for? He was generating flames of heat, tremors of desire, just holding her this way, and he hadn't even touched his lips to hers yet.

"Umm, I hate to break it to you, Cisco, but this is not making me feel safe," Gillian commented as he lifted the soft veil of her hair and kissed his way down the exposed line of her throat to the U of her collarbone.

Cisco bent his head and, taking advantage of the languid ribbon of desire spreading through her, kissed her full on the mouth, until her toes curled and a hot flush swept through her entire body. She gulped in air, aware of the tantalizing feel of solid muscle and satin skin, and lower still, the heated stirrings of his desire. "Then what will?" he teased softly, holding her still as he kissed her again, even more thoroughly this time.

Unable to help herself, Gillian began to yield, then caught herself and moaned low in the back of her throat. "Cisco—" She splayed her hands across his bare chest, her fingers sliding through the thick mat of chest hair to the warm smooth muscle beneath. But it was too late; he was already undoing the buttons on her pajama top. Tendrils of white heat swept through her as his mouth moved sensually on the hollow between her breasts, then returned with devastating slowness to her mouth.

"Want me to stop?" he whispered as he deepened the kiss and slipped his hand inside to cup the soft curve of her breast.

Gillian moaned as his fingertips closed over her

nipple, massaging it into a point. The pleasure was almost unbearable as everything around her went soft and fuzzy except the hot, hard pressure of his mouth. She knew all the reasons why they shouldn't consummate this marriage, yet she had the urge to surrender completely to his tender touch and slow, sensuous kiss. "Yes. No. I don't know...."

"Well, while you're thinking about it..." He stroked his way down her spine, his caressing fingertips every bit as sure and sensual and somehow comforting as his kiss. "Think about this." He spoke as his tongue moved across her lips. "And this." His lips moved to her breast as his thigh moved between hers, easing her legs apart, as he moved to possess her the way only a husband could.

Heat curled high and low. She felt her back arching off the bed even as his hands found her, too. Heavy and warm, they splayed across her skin, slipped across her abdomen, moved lower still.

For long glorious moments she gave herself up to the tension building inside her. For so long she had wanted to forget, and now she was. His kisses, his touch, the warm sensuality of their embrace combined to wipe out everything sordid and ugly that had gone before.

It had been so long since she had been touched, held...so long since she had let herself want, she thought as a new wave of heat and longing washed over her.

What was it Max had said? she wondered as she

felt herself spinning into oblivion. *Reach out with both hands and grab the happiness that is waiting for you.* That, she thought fiercely, her mind made up, was what she was going to do tonight. They might only be married for a couple days...their union might only amount to a fling, but right this moment they were husband and wife and she was going to enjoy it while it lasted.

Cisco hadn't planned for this to happen. He hadn't expected to do anything but protect Gillian and help her find a way out of whatever trouble she was in. But now that she was here, cosseted in his arms, now that she beginning to confide in him, he found he had a different agenda entirely. He wanted to take the kind of risks he'd never yet dared and make Gillian his own in every way that counted. He wanted to offer her the safety and security her previous life had lacked. Not just for tonight, but for the entire forty-eight hours and beyond....

The fact they were playing into Max's matchmaking plan bothered him a little, Cisco thought as he continued to kiss and caress Gillian with a slow deliberateness that was as tantalizing to him as it was to her.

He did not like being manipulated into anything, even if it was allegedly something that was destined to be. But deeper than his concern over Max's bold machinations was his hunger to know everything about her.

Gillian had cloaked herself in mystery, and that

mystery extended to the way she responded to his kisses, with a sweet, demanding need that soon burst into flame. With the way she touched him, so sweetly and tenderly. And with the way she opened herself to his possession, letting him take charge, then surprising him again as she arched up wantonly to meet him, thrust for thrust.

She embraced him like a woman who had been too long without affection…without closeness of any kind. But that was ending, he decided as he deepened his strokes and urged her on to soaring heights. And it was ending now.

Because Gillian wasn't alone any longer, and neither was he. They had each other, and they had this. And for the moment, he thought as his heart pounded and there was no more holding back, this was enough.

Gillian pulled him closer, holding him tight against the softness of her breasts, her response honest and uncompromising and unashamed.

He felt her tremble as she reached the frenzied acceleration to climax, felt her draw him into the white-hot pleasure of it all, and then he, too, was free-falling into oblivion, shuddering with release, and plummeting over the edge.

CISCO HELD HER until the trembling stopped and their breathing finally slowed, then moved back to look into her eyes. Rushing into a love affair was definitely not his style, but what the heck, he figured. The two of them were old enough, and adult enough, to be able to handle it.

"I just can't believe it," Gillian murmured in a stunned voice as she ducked her head shyly and stroked her hands across his chest.

"Can't believe what?" Cisco asked, still holding her close.

She sighed serenely as she wreathed her arms about his neck and continued to snuggle in his arms. "I do feel safe when you hold me like this."

Cisco felt a deep satisfaction, too, at simply being with her this way. A satisfaction Max would have gloried knowing about. Irritated, Cisco pushed the disturbing thought away. Max was his mentor, friend and father figure all rolled into one, but he was not doing any of this to please Max. Nor had he done it because Gillian needed saving. He had made love to her because it had felt right. It was as simple and honest and uncomplicated as that. "Maybe Max is right. Maybe we do belong together long-term," he told her.

Without warning, the troubled light was back in her eyes.

"Cisco!" she exclaimed, distressed. "You can't believe that," Gillian whispered back, studying him even more intently.

It was almost as if, Cisco thought, she were searching for the trap in his words. Wanting…needing…to comfort her once again, Cisco framed her face with his hands and tilted her face up to his. "All I know for certain is that I want you," he told her victoriously, deciding for now to stick with the fact they were sexually compatible. "It's as simple and complicated as that."

"Yes, it is," Gillian agreed in a soft, serious voice, surprising him once again as she leaned up and warmly and seductively pressed her lips to his. "Because heaven help me, Cisco Kidd, I want you, too."

Chapter Six

"You know, as warm and cozy as that was, I don't think we should sleep together again," Gillian said first thing the following morning as she extricated herself from the rumpled covers on the sofa bed.

Given Gillian's skittish nature, Cisco had half expected she might pull back from their newfound intimacy, once they faced the light of day. "Why not?" he asked casually as he watched her shrug into his pajama top and button up the front.

Gillian began to look a little panicked as she finished her task and pivoted away from him. "Isn't it obvious? It's too intimate."

"Too intimate," Cisco repeated, remembering how warm and pliant her mouth had been beneath his.

"Yes." Her emotions under tight control once again, Gillian raked a hand through her auburn hair. While Cisco scrambled around for his pajama pants, she headed for the kitchen and came back with a tall glass of orange juice for each of them. Their fingers brushed as she handed him the glass. "The lovemaking was great, I won't deny that—"

"Good," Cisco said, because he wasn't about to deny that, either.

Gillian pressed the rim of her glass against lips that were still swollen from his kisses. She met his eyes in a forthright manner, then shrugged as she explained matter-of-factly, "I just hadn't anticipated the way waking and finding myself in your arms would make me feel."

Or the way she would look now, Cisco thought, all soft and tousled and warm. Not to mention well loved. Unhappily, the physical and emotional well-being that came from two heated lovemaking sessions and several hours of contented sleep were obviously not what she was referring to.

Cisco rolled to his feet and moved forward languidly until they stood toe-to-toe. He looked down at her. "And how exactly does sleeping with me make you feel, Gillian?" he asked gently, aware it was all he could do not to put his juice glass aside, take her into his arms again and kiss her doubts away.

Gillian sighed and looked even more skittish as she backed away. "Like we're really married."

"What's wrong with that?" Cisco gave her a cocky grin that belied the hurt in his words.

"Everything," Gillian declared with a rush of emotion that surprised him as she turned and headed for the bathroom, Cisco trailing her. "Because our marriage isn't a real one, Cisco. It's a business arrangement." She looked at herself in the mirror and frowned.

All too aware of how little she had on beneath his pajama top, and how little it would take to persuade him to make love to her again, Cisco reminded her, "*Businesslike* is not a word I would use to describe the way you were acting last night."

A fiery blush deepened the color across her cheeks. Gillian avoided his glance completely as she busied herself checking out the supply of shampoo, soap and toothpaste on the medicine cabinet shelves. "You know as well as I do what all that was about."

Maybe. Maybe not. Cisco remained in the open bathroom doorway. His eyes searched hers. "I'd be interested to hear your version."

Gillian blew out an exasperated breath, looking supremely irritated he was forcing her to spell it out for them. "It had obviously been a while for me since I'd...well, you know—"

"Made love. And it had been a while for both of us, Gillian," Cisco corrected gently, not bothered by that at all. What was bothering him was the soft movement of her breasts beneath the pajama top and the sleek sexiness of her bare legs.

He'd barely been awake ten minutes and already his whole body was aching to possess her again, and his heart...well, to his chagrin, that was in no better shape.

To his amazement, it didn't seem to matter she was pushing him away with both hands, now that she'd had time to think about the new turn in their relationship. He only knew he was drawn to her as he had never been drawn to anyone else. And that was something he feared was not going to change no matter how this spur-of-the-moment marriage of theirs did or did not work out.

With a deep bolstering breath, Gillian picked up the hairbrush on the sink and, facing forward, began to run it through her hair. "The fact of the matter is we both wanted what happened last night to happen," Gillian continued determinedly, meeting his eyes in the mirror. "And so it did. And now that it has, and our…basic curiosity about each other has been satisfied, it won't happen again."

Just when he thought he understood her, she threw him for a loop. "You really think that's what last night was about, just satisfying our curiosity?" Cisco echoed, shocked. He'd never been accused of being overly sentimental; it surprised him how much the hours they'd shared had meant to him. Furthermore, in his view, curiosity had had very little to do with what happened. It had been about passion, desire, attraction, needing each other—and about a shared loneliness that went soul deep.

Her composure intact, Gillian lifted her slender shoulders in an insouciant shrug. "That, and maybe getting rid of the leftover adrenaline simmering in our veins," she told him practically as she finished restoring order to her wildly curling mane of red hair.

Laying the brush down, she turned to face him once

again. "You have to admit we were both pretty pumped, after I pulled a gun on you. But that won't happen again, either. So we shouldn't have anything to worry about during the next thirty-six hours."

Or anything else that would prompt them to fall recklessly into each other's arms, Cisco figured she meant. And though that should have been as much a comfort to him as it was to her, as he was no more prone to indulge in reckless love affairs than she, it wasn't. Time was passing much more quickly than he had imagined it would. He couldn't deny at first he had wished the forty-eight hours would hurry up and pass. Now he was wishing he could slow down the clock. Draw out each and every minute. And that had little to do with the truth he was trying to whittle out of her and everything to do with wanting to spend time with her.

Wise or not, he wanted to make love to her again. Not hotly and passionately, as he had last night, but slowly and tenderly this time. Afterward, he wanted to cradle her in his arms and hold her close. He wanted her to fall asleep in his arms, and be happy about it—instead of skittish—when she woke again and found herself in his arms.

She shrugged as if that ended the conversation. "Anyway, as they say, there's no use crying over spilled milk. So if you don't mind..." She picked up the toothbrush he had lent her the night before and put toothpaste on it.

Her indifference was no more convincing than her

bravado had been, but for the heck of it, Cisco decided to play along anyway.

"Of course there were other reasons, as well, why that happened last night, don't forget," he said, reminding himself sternly of the real reason he'd let Max push him into this marriage. So he could get close enough to Gillian to really help her. He opened the linen closet to get two fresh towels and a washcloth for her.

"Really," Gillian countered as she accepted the linens he handed her. "And what would that be?" she asked, then went back to brushing her teeth.

"Making love with me was a pretty effective way to change the subject away from the nightmares you still have about your dangerous past." Cisco put toothpaste on his toothbrush, too.

Gillian stiffened indignantly as she rinsed her mouth. "I did not seduce you as a way of changing the subject, Cisco Kidd!"

Finished, Cisco rinsed his toothbrush and put it back in the holder. "Nor did I seduce you last night." He met Gillian's eyes in the mirror, wondering if she knew how sexy she looked clad in the oversize pajama top. "It was a mutual combustion of heat and passion that brought us together," he finished smugly.

Gillian's cheeks flushed. "Not to mention the fact that I was shaken up by a nightmare about my past."

"A past you still haven't told me much about," he pointed out, glad she had brought that up.

Silence fell between them, more telling than any

lies, or the upset way she had reacted when Pete Lloyd had appeared to recognize her at the wedding.

Gillian glared at him as she turned on the warm water and lathered up a bar of soap. "I told you everything I could," she declared hotly as she began to wash her face.

"Everything?" Cisco echoed, his expression hardening as he watched her cover her face with silky bubbles. "I don't think so, Gillian." As an attorney, he had learned when a client was holding back, and Gillian was still holding back plenty. But he also sensed she had revealed far more to him than she normally did. And that it bothered her that she had confided in him even as much as she had.

Gillian shrugged, again making light of what had just happened between them the previous night. She bent over the sink, the pajama top riding high on the backs of her slender thighs, as she splashed warm water on her face. "If you're expecting any more 'true confessions' from me, Cisco, you're going to be waiting an awfully long time," she told him succinctly as she blotted her face dry. "Because day or night, I have nothing more to say to you on that subject."

Ditto for the whole truth and nothing but the truth, he thought, as she flattened a hand on his chest and directed him out of the bathroom. "I do, however, need to borrow something besides your pajamas to wear."

"Guess you can't go around in my pajamas all day."

"Guess not," she agreed dryly.

"Nor would a wedding dress do."

"Right again."

Cisco strolled to his closet, followed by Gillian. "Knowing Max, more clothes for you—probably ranching duds—are on the way. In the meantime, you can have your pick of my shirts. This blue one here—" he handed her one in pale blue "—might look nice."

She held it up to her, noting as she did that it came down to midthigh on her. "It'll be fine. I'll just roll up the sleeves. About pants of some sort—"

"I've got some workout shorts with a drawstring waist." He plucked them out of his bureau. "Think these will do?"

Gillian held up the soft gray jersey to her, noting the hem fell just above her knee. "Yes, thank you."

"White crew socks to go with your sneakers." Cisco handed her a pair of those, too. "But I don't have any lingerie." Nor would he mind if she continued to go without.

But alas, he realized quickly, that also was not to be. "Relax. I'll hand-wash my unmentionables while I'm in the shower. They're mostly lace anyway, so they'll only take a minute to dry if you have a hair dryer I can use."

Cisco swallowed. "The dryer's in the drawer next to the sink."

"Thanks." Gillian slipped back into the bathroom. A split second later, the lock turned. The shower began to run.

Knowing he'd better find something to busy himself with while she was in the shower—if he didn't want to get aroused all over again, just thinking about her standing naked under the spray—Cisco went into the kitchen, made coffee and poured himself another glass of juice. For the first time he wished he knew how to cook something—anything. And that he kept some sort of food, other than a few beverages, in his apartment.

He was finishing his first cup of coffee and thinking about whether they should go to Pearl's for breakfast or hit the supermarket for supplies, when the phone rang. Cisco picked up on the second ring.

"Hey, Cisco!" Trace's teenage son Nate teased. "How does it feel to be famous?"

Cisco grinned, kicked back in his chair and wondered what mischief Trace and Susannah's four boys were in now. "What are you talking about?" Cisco asked.

"*USA Daily.* Parts of the Monday edition of the newspaper are already posted on the Internet."

Cisco knew there'd been several journalists at the wedding. "Let me guess," Cisco drawled, already switching on his computer and logging on to the Internet. "They wrote an article about Max being alive after all, and mentioned me as the attorney who carried out Max's wishes and arranged all the shenanigans.''

"Well, yeah, they did that," Nate affirmed cheerfully, "but that's not why your picture's in the paper.''

Cisco typed in the newspaper's address and waited impatiently for the information to appear on-screen.

"You're in there because you and Gillian got married last night." Nate paused. "The article's on the front page of the Lifestyle section.''

The color photo booted up and it was all Cisco could do not to groan as he saw his own image on the screen. "I see it.''

"Okay, just remember I told you first!" Nate said.

"I will. Thanks, Nate.''

Gillian emerged from the bedroom, towel drying her hair. She looked concerned. "What's up?''

"This.'' Cisco pointed to his computer screen.

Gillian leaned over his shoulder and looked at a news photo of a bride and groom exchanging wedding rings. "Wedding Fever Sweeps The Nation.'' Gillian read the headline out loud. "'From the traditional wedding to the—' *oh my God!*'' She clutched his shoulders tightly as the enormity of what had happened sunk in. "Is that us?''

"In living color," Cisco replied dryly.

"And they've identified us both by name!" Gillian began to pace.

"That is customary.''

She spun around and stomped back to the computer. The color draining from her face, she stared intently at the posted news article, reading aloud the caption beneath the photo. "'Caught up in the excitement of a triple wedding, logging camp chef Gillian Taylor marries Fort Benton attorney Cisco Kidd in a spur-of-the-moment marriage ceremony on the Silver Spur Ranch in Montana....'" She shook her head and paled all the more. "Is this on the stands now?"

"It's on the Internet now," he explained, using his index finger to point out the time and date of the posting. "It's been there since 1:28 this morning, or roughly six hours now. It'll be on the newsstands Monday morning."

"Well, that's impossible!" She looked at him, wild-eyed, distressed. "Cisco, you've got to do something to stop it!"

"I can't."

"Why not?" Gillian paced away from him. "You're a lawyer! We never gave permission for our photos to be used."

Cisco sat back in his chair. "Under current law, we don't have to," he said calmly. "Consent is only required for commercial use of a photo. News photos, on the other hand, require no consent."

Gillian paled as she trod nearer in a drift of flowery perfume. She splayed a hand across her chest. "We're news?"

Cisco nodded grimly. Though he sensed they felt the way they did for very different reasons, this wasn't what he wanted, either. "We became news when we married the way we did."

Gillian dragged a chair over and sank into it, so they were sitting face-to-face. "Can't we ask them to pull the photo?" Gillian asked in desperation.

Cisco regarded Gillian patiently. He wasn't above using this situation to get more of the information he needed from her, particularly when she wouldn't allow him to help her any other way. "For what reason?"

Gillian waved her arms at him in exasperation, punctuating each and every word she spoke. "Because I don't want to be famous."

The question was why didn't she want to be famous. What else was she running from? What had Pete Lloyd, from Kansas, started to recall last night that had thrown her into a panic?

Cisco called on his experience as an attorney to reassure her gently. "Fame like this fades more quickly than you can imagine."

Gillian's soft lips tightened into a rebellious line. "So, in other words you're telling me we're stuck with that article, and that Monday morning it's going to be on every newsstand in America?"

Cisco nodded grimly, taking in the decidedly militant edge to her posture. "Looks like, yes."

GILLIAN COULDN'T BELIEVE it. Ten years on the run. Ten years of holding everyone, save Susannah McKendrick and her boys, at arm's length. The moment she put her fear of being discovered aside and decided to do something for herself, like marry Cisco to gain a new legal name, a permanent home on the ranch and a business, what should happen but her past comes back to haunt her with a vengeance! First in the form of former KSU professor Pete Lloyd at last night's wedding, thinking she looked somehow familiar to him, and now this!

"You're upset?" Cisco guessed as he continued to study her with concern etching his features.

The time to be coy had passed. "Hell, yes, I'm upset, Cisco. Damned upset. Suppose other papers pick this up?" she asked emotionally.

"I'll be honest with you. Chances of killing such a lively human-interest story are almost nil, particularly when the story has already been posted on-line."

Almost, but not absolutely. "But we could try, couldn't we?"

"Yes, but there's no guarantee our efforts would be successful. And we can't do anything about the six hours the story has already been on-line."

Beggars couldn't be choosers, Gillian thought. At this point, she'd take what she could get. "What about the photo of us?" she asked anxiously. "Can we do anything about that?"

Cisco frowned. "Again, we can't stop it because it's news, but we could try and purchase the copyright, and hence control the distribution of the said photo from now on. I'm warning you, though. Doing something like this'll be an expensive proposition."

Gillian sighed her relief. "I don't care. I'll pay you back every cent, I swear. I just want my—I mean our—photo off the Internet."

Cisco narrowed his eyes at her appraisingly. "All right," Cisco said finally. "I'll see what I can do."

"IT'S DONE," Cisco said a tense hour and a half later. "The copyright on the photo is ours. Any mention of our wedding is being stricken from the article, but *USA Daily* is going to continue with the modified article on the triple wedding at the Silver Spur."

"So there'll be no mention of our names or photo of us in the *USA Daily* newspaper that hits the stands tomorrow morning?" Gillian asked.

"Correct."

"Oh, thank heavens."

Cisco continued to study her, looking as though he wanted to ask her so much, but—his expression turning protective—didn't. "Are you okay?" was all he said.

Gillian nodded. Now that their names and photos were off the Internet, she felt a lot better.

Deciding she needed a time-out rather than risk any further questions, however, Gillian sent him a bracing smile. "I think we both need something to eat. If it's all right with you, I'd like to take our first time-out and walk down to the twenty-four-hour supermarket and get some food for breakfast."

"You don't have to cook," Cisco pointed out as Gillian braided her hair into a loose plait over one shoulder, and fastened it with a coated elastic band. "We could eat at Pearl's."

"It's no problem." Gillian waved off his concern. "I want to do it. Besides, cooking relaxes me." And right now, Gillian thought, as she picked up her purse and headed toward the shiny black revolver on the table, she needed to relax.

Cisco frowned as she picked the gun up and carefully replaced it in her purse.

Ignoring his faint look of disapproval, Gillian closed her purse and inquired cheerfully, "Any preferences for breakfast?"

Cisco shook his head and continued watching her as though he knew something was up and it was just a matter of time until he found out precisely what that was. "Whatever you want is fine with me," he said.

CISCO WAITED until Gillian had left, then sat down behind the desk and, putting off his shower for a few more minutes, telephoned the head of the detective agency Max owned on the West Coast. "Lynda, Cisco Kidd. Sorry I woke you."

"What's up?" she asked around a yawn while a male voice grumbled sleepily in the background. "It must be important for you to be calling me at this hour."

"Yeah, it is," Cisco admitted, leaning back in his leather swivel chair. "I've got someone I need you to check out for me. Her name is Gillian Taylor. She used to work as a chef in L.A., mostly for Trace's wife, Susannah Hart.''

"What's this Ms. Gillian Taylor done to warrant your interest?" Lynda asked curiously.

"She agreed to be my wife." He went on to give a skeletal synopsis of the events of the past twelve-plus hours. *And I am now more certain than ever she needs help the way I once did.* "My gut feeling is that she's running from someone or something, 'cause she's damn near hysterical about her picture appearing in the Monday edition of the *USA Daily* newspaper." Briefly, Cisco explained what lengths he'd gone to to have the picture and article pulled, then concluded, "She's also carrying a gun on a regular basis.''

"Uh-oh.''

"Uh-oh's right. She also claims to have once been a student at UCLA, but they have no record of her.''

Cisco heard Lynda scrambling for a paper and a pen. "Did you ask her why not?" Lynda asked.

"She claims they've lost her records.''

"You don't buy it?''

Cisco frowned. "I don't know. I have a feeling she's only told me a very small portion of what she's running from, and I know from her reaction this morning and last night that she still feels she could be in rather immediate danger. Since she won't confide in me further, at least at this point, I'm going to have to look into the reasons for her fear myself." It was the only way he could help and protect her.

"I understand where you're coming from," Lynda sympathized.

Cisco sighed inwardly. The question was would Gillian, if she ever found out what he'd done in having her investigated? "You might also look to see if there were any police complaints filed by her against someone named Phillip for breaking and entering or stalking."

"Any idea where or when these incidents might have taken place?"

Cisco hazarded a guess. "Try looking in the Midwest, probably Kansas, ten years or so ago."

"I presume there's a rush on this?"

"You bet your bottom dollar there is," Cisco said. Before he even knew what they were facing, his gut told him danger could be upon them. And that could be deadly, for both of them.

"I TOLD YOU THEY'D BE UP," Cody said after Gillian had opened the door to Max's nephew and his new bride, Callie.

"We are, but Cisco is in the shower." Gillian peered at them. She was still breathless from her under-thirty minute run to the Fort Benton grocery. Thankfully, Cisco lived in town, as opposed to out on the ranch, and the twenty-four-hour grocery was just down the street, otherwise it would've been impossible. "Aren't you two supposed to be on your honeymoon?" she asked the cowboy and his beautiful, blond bride.

Cody and Callie McKendrick grinned in unison and wrapped their arms around each other. "We delayed it for a few days on account of we promised Uncle Max we'd help get you and Cisco together," Callie explained, her green eyes sparkling warmly.

Cody took off his hat and raked a hand through his shoulder-length wheat blond hair, which was tied back with a rawhide strip. "We owe Max and Cisco a lot, since they both did so much to bring Callie and me back together," Cody said. "Normally, of course, I don't think interfering is a good thing, but in this case, 'cause Cisco's been so much like a brother to me, I'd be willing to make an exception. And besides—" Cody paused to kiss the top of Callie's head "—if anyone around here deserves to be happy, Cisco does."

Gillian was beginning to agree with that. "How do you know I make him happy?" Gillian asked curiously.

Cody and Callie exchanged speculative looks, rife with romance. "All anyone had to do was look at the sparks flying between you last night to know there's something special there," Callie said.

"Besides," Cody added as he tightened his arm around his wife's waist, "Cisco wouldn't have said 'I do,' even on the spur of the moment, unless he was really interested in you."

Gillian flushed, wondering if that was true.

Callie turned to Cody and toyed with the buttons on his shirt. As usual, she was dressed in jeans, vest and shirt and her red cowgirl boots. "Now that we know someone is here, don't you think we should bring in the things we have for Gillian and Cisco?" Callie asked.

"Right," Cody said.

Looking reluctant to be apart from his new bride even for just a second, Cody nevertheless took off down the stairs. "What do you have for us?" Gillian asked Callie curiously, knowing that Max could be very generous indeed.

"Beats me," Callie said. She noticed on the kitchen counter the groceries that Gillian had yet to put away. "Max was typically enigmatic."

Cody returned carrying a stack of gaily wrapped presents and a single envelope, just as a fully dressed, shaven and showered Cisco Kidd emerged from the bathroom. He was wearing a white Western shirt, open at the throat, soft faded jeans and boots. He looked handsome and at ease in the casual rancher's clothing. "What's going on?" Cisco asked cheerfully, joining the group.

Cody set the presents in front of Gillian, and handed Cisco the single envelope. "Presents for the two of you, from Max."

Callie looked from Gillian to Cisco. She took the time to study them intently. "Everything going okay for the two of you so far?" She hesitated for a moment. "I mean, you're getting along and everything, aren't you?" Callie continued, concerned.

You mean beside the fact we threw caution to the

wind and recklessly made love twice during the night?
Gillian thought wryly. She still wasn't sure what had
come over her, if it was the romance of the evening,
or wedding fever, or just the fact she'd been alone
and on the run for so long now. She only knew that
when Cisco held her, she felt safe. And when he
kissed her, and made love to her with such fiery passion, she felt whole again, as though she had a future
not just here on the ranch, but with him.

And then there was the potentially disastrous situation with their photo on the Internet. He had handled
that just right, putting some pressure on her of course
to level with him, but not pushing her too hard just
the same.

She didn't know how he did it, exactly. She just
knew whenever he was by her side she felt everything
really would be all right. Maybe not today exactly,
but someday. And that, Gillian admitted, was a feeling she did not want to relinquish, even though, because the *USA Daily* news photo had been posted on
the Internet she might soon have to do so.

"Everything's fine," Gillian finally answered as
they exchanged a glance, standing united on that
front.

What had happened between the two of them—the
fact they'd decided on the spur of the moment to em-
bark on a wild, reckless weekend love affair—was
nobody's business but their own, Gillian thought.

Cody and Callie exchanged looks rife with both

disbelief and humor. "Uh-huh. Well, if you need us, you know how to find us," Cody drawled.

"See you," Callie echoed with a grin and wave.

Their eyes dancing with hopelessly romantic lights, the newlyweds were off.

Cisco shut the door after them and inclined his head at the ribbon-wrapped boxes. "Aren't you going to open them?" he asked Gillian.

Gillian had to admit she was curious. "It's probably too much to hope he's giving back the things of mine he put in storage, isn't it?"

Cisco shrugged as she tugged at a ribbon. "With Max, you never know."

The first box contained a very beautiful, very sexy floor-length negligee in emerald green lace. Gillian blushed at the thought Max had expected—correctly, it turned out—for them to end up making love in no time flat. Was the chemistry between she and Cisco really that obvious? And if so, what did it mean? Deciding not to think about that for the moment, she put the negligee aside.

"Going to model it for me now?" Cisco teased.

"You wish," Gillian replied as she simultaneously flushed with pleasure and ignored the hint of renewed sexual interest in Cisco's eyes. Besides, she much prefered wearing just the soft flannel top to Cisco's cowboy pajamas, she told herself defiantly. No way was she wearing that negligee.

"Want me to help you open the rest?" Cisco

teased, edging nearer. The hint of sandalwood and sage clung to his freshly shaven jaw.

"No, thanks," Gillian replied. She still wanted first glimpse. Because if it was too much, this time it was not coming all the way out of the box!

But to her relief, Max's second gift to her was much more practical. "What is that? A denim skirt?" Cisco asked.

"A split skirt, the kind specifically made for sitting astride a horse. And a tailored blue denim blouse to go with it." Reassured, and happy—for now she had something to wear today aside from Cisco's clothing or her wedding dress—Gillian tackled the rest of the boxes in short order. Finding a flat-brimmed hat to protect her from the sun, a pair of pine green Western boots, more jeans and a pretty plaid shirt and a whole boxful of satin undergarments and cotton socks, suitable for wearing with her new boots. There was also a handwritten note addressed to Gillian.

"Just a few things to tide you over 'til you reach the honeymoon cottage," Max had written, "where even more treasures...of all kinds...await."

Feeling both perplexed and wary, Gillian handed the note over for Cisco to see. "What do you suppose this means?" she asked curiously.

Cisco shrugged, his silver-gray eyes still holding hers. "I don't know. We'll have to go out there and find out." He cut a glance at the groceries still out.

"When?" Gillian asked, getting up and heading for

the kitchen, just as there was another knock at the door.

"As soon as possible," Cisco replied as he moved to answer the door while she went on into the kitchen.

There, outside the door, was Pearl, a picnic basket slung over her arm.

"What are you doing out so early?" Cisco asked. Usually Pearl let her staff handle the breakfast rush, while she ruled the diner during the lunch and dinner hours.

"Oh, I couldn't sleep, so I thought I'd make myself useful and make you two lovebirds something to eat, since I know you don't keep much of anything in your refrigerator." Pearl handed over the wicker basket and looked at him closely. "You two *are* getting along, aren't you?"

That all depends, Cisco thought, on how you defined "getting along." If that meant being at loggerheads one minute, making wild passionate love the next, they were getting along splendidly. But not about to go into that with even a dear old friend, he peered inside the basket at the goodies she'd packed. "Your timing is great, Pearl. Gillian and I were just opening a few presents from Max and getting ready to go out to the honeymoon cottage."

Pearl cast a glance at the presents scattered across the sofa. She looked anything but pleased. "That buzzard still thinks he can buy his way out of everything, doesn't he?" Pearl muttered, planting both hands on her hips.

"I take it this means you're still mad at him," Gillian called sympathetically from the kitchen, where she was busy putting away the groceries she had purchased.

"You bet I am," Pearl replied, as she sashayed in to sit at the breakfast counter opposite Gillian. "You have my sympathies, Gillian, to be wrapped in another of Max's crazy schemes. Though I must admit I can't feel bad he is trying to get you married off, Cisco."

Cisco gave Pearl an odd look as he joined them. "Why?"

"Well, you know... You had such a rough childhood and all.... I just want to see you happy and with someone instead of spending your life all alone."

Cisco strode past Pearl and poured himself another cup of coffee, irked at the unexpected display of pity. "I don't need your sympathy, Pearl," he said gruffly as he poured her a cup of coffee, too.

"Honey, I know you don't." Pearl stirred in two lumps of sugar. "But you've got it anyway." Giving Cisco no chance to respond, Pearl grinned and inclined her head at the discarded cowboy pajamas. "Ahh, now, who's been wearing these?" she teased.

"I have," Cisco and Gillian said in unison.

Blushing, Gillian poured herself a cup of coffee and leaned against the opposite counter as she went on to admit, "Actually, thanks to Max's machinations, we were a little short on clothes last night, so we split them. Cisco wore the bottoms, I wore the top.''

''Hmm.'' Pearl grinned mischieviously, as if thinking the worst.

Cisco held up a palm. ''Now, Pearl, it wasn't like that,'' Cisco said.

At least it hadn't started out that way when they had made the decision to each wear a part of the pajamas, Gillian agreed. They had done so with the most conservative of intentions. It was only her bad dream…and his kindness…and the intimacy of the moment…plus their proximity to each other that had led to the lovemaking.

''Well, I bet the two of you were both cute as buttons anyway,'' Pearl said as she waggled a finger at Cisco teasingly.

''Okay, Pearl, enough reminiscing.'' He held up a staying hand as a flush started in his neck and climbed to his cheeks.

''All right, I can see I'm embarrassing you,'' Pearl said with a careless wave of her hand. ''So I'll be on my way.''

''Sure you wouldn't like to stay and have some breakfast with us?'' Gillian asked, suddenly determined not to be alone with Cisco.

''No thanks, honey.'' Pearl gave her an officious smile as she patted the pins in her upswept hair, making sure it was still neatly in place. With her voice dropping a confiding notch, she said, ''The upset way I've been feeling since I tangled with that rascally old beau of mine, I couldn't eat a bite. In fact, if you want to know the truth, my temper is still as hot as a two-dollar pistol.''

"Speaking of the rascal, have you talked to Max?'' Cisco interjected.

"No,'' Pearl said, her chin setting stubbornly, ''and I don't want to, either. So you can save your advice for someone who wants to hear it.''

Cisco fell in step beside Pearl as he walked her to the door. "The two of you have been together an awfully long time.''

"Too long." Pearl sighed with heartfelt chagrin. "It's time I moved on to greener pastures, or at least to someone who loves and trusts me enough to confide in—and marry—me.''

Concern etched deep lines around the corners of Cisco's lips as he held Pearl up at the door. "Does Max know how you feel?'' he asked.

"He darn well should,'' Pearl replied stubbornly. "And I don't care if he doesn't.'' The discussion was finished, as far as she was concerned, and she slipped out before another word could be said.

Gillian, who had joined them at the door to the apartment, was silent a moment. She turned to Cisco, fighting a wave of unbearable sadness. Maybe it was overly sentimental of her, but she hated it when people let happiness slip through their fingers, and from what she had seen when she first arrived in town three weeks ago, Pearl and Max had really seemed to belong together. "Maybe it's time Max had a little of his own medicine," Gillian suggested dryly.

Cisco's gray eyes lit with interest. "What are you suggesting?"

Gillian grinned and linked hands with Cisco. "That we forget ourselves for a while and turn our talents to matchmaking, too."

"WHAT DO YOU MEAN they won't come for lunch?" Gillian demanded as Cisco joined her in the kitchen of his apartment.

"Just that. They both said no."

Gillian bit her lip. "Think we were too obvious?"

"Probably." Cisco fell silent. "We'll never get them back together if we can't get them off somewhere alone long enough to talk."

"Any ideas?"

Cisco stroked his jaw thoughtfully. "Well, now that you mention it, Max does have that Silver Streak recreational vehicle. It's as luxurious as they come and is rigged to be driven just about anywhere." Cisco's smile spread. "I know just the place to park it, too. Not too far from Trace and Susannah's place, there's a beautiful campsite next to the lake."

"Sounds good, but how are we going to get them in it?"

Cisco snapped his fingers. "By enlisting some comrades they'd never suspect." He reached for the phone.

"Who are you calling?"

He smiled mysteriously. "You'll see."

"Okay, everyone set?" Cisco asked Trace and Susannah McKendrick's four rambunctious boys.

"I'll call Pearl and tell her we need a baby-sitter so Mom and Dad can have some time alone," ten-year-old Jason said.

"I'll call Max and tell him the same thing," eight-year-old Mickey added.

"We'll ask Uncle Max to show up thirty minutes early and do some fishing down by the lake," sixteen-year-old Scott said.

"When Pearl shows up, we'll give a whistle signal and get her busy in the RV, and then get Max to come back up here," fourteen-year-old Nate concluded.

"He and Pearl will be really ticked off when they find out we tricked 'em," Mickey continued.

"While they're yelling at each other, we'll all take off and leave 'em stranded here at the campsite," Jason said.

"Yeah, and before you know it, they'll be all kissy-face again," Mickey concluded impishly.

"Indeed." Gillian smiled.

The next hour everything went like clockwork. Both Max and Pearl happily agreed to baby-sit the boys. Max showed up with the RV. He parked it at the campsite and then he and the boys promptly went off to fish while Gillian and Cisco crept back and put the finishing touches inside: flowers, candles, wine, soft music and a delicious lunch.

Finished, they tiptoed out of the RV and into the nearby woods and waited. And waited. And waited. And still no Pearl.

"What could be keeping her?" Gillian whispered anxiously as she paced back and forth, being careful to keep out of sight.

"Heck if I know." Cisco looked around. "She's usually very punctual."

Gillian looked toward the lake, a short distance away beyond the trees. "Max and the boys are awfully quiet."

Cisco grimaced. "They're fishing. They're supposed to be quiet."

Gillian rolled her eyes. "Those boys are never that quiet unless they're getting in trouble."

Cisco and Gillian exchanged looks. "Oh, my—"

"You don't think—"

Cisco swore. Simultaneously, they raced down the leaf-strewn path to the lake. To their chagrin, where the boys should have been was a red bandanna tied to a stick and waving in the gentle summer breeze. A note written on Silver Spur stationery was pinned to that.

"'Dear Cisco and Gillian,'" Cisco read aloud. "'Nice try, but Pearl and I saw your machinations a mile away. No need to let the next few hours go to waste, though. The distributor caps to your car and my RV will be returned to you this afternoon around two.'" Cisco sighed. "It's signed by both Max and Pearl. And down here is another note—looks like it's from the boys. It says, 'Sorry, guys, but they paid us more than you.' And all four of them have signed that.''

Gillian didn't know whether to chuckle or cry. She tipped the brim of her hat back. ''So, we've been double-crossed,'' she concluded wearily.

''Apparently.''

Gillian released an exasperated breath, and thought back to the distributor cap remark. She narrowed her glance at Cisco. ''We really are stuck, then?''

Cisco grimaced, swept off his Stetson and shoved a hand through his hair. ''What do you think?''

''How DOES THIS SPOT LOOK to you?'' Cisco asked Gillian as they stopped next to a flower-filled meadow at the base of Silver Ridge Mountain. Trees surrounded the golden field on all four sides. In one direction a rushing mountain stream gleamed as blue as the sky overhead in the early-afternoon sunlight, in the other the Silver Streak RV was plainly in view.

''It looks great,'' Gillian said quietly. A lot less intimate than the RV.

Together, they spread out a blanket on the soft warm grass beneath the spreading branches of a large oak tree. The two of them settled on the blanket. Cisco watched while Gillian began bringing out the sumptuously prepared food they'd intended for Pearl and Max.

''You're really taking this in stride,'' Cisco said as

he helped himself to a slab of country ham and a serving of fresh, sliced fruit.

Gillian filled her own plate to overflowing. "It's not like we can do anything about being stuck out here, so we might as well enjoy our day off."

"Do you enjoy your work as a chef?" Cisco asked, watching the sunlight catch her hair and turn it into amber fire.

Oblivious to his urge to run his hands through the wildly curling ends of her hair, Gillian nodded. "Usually, although when you work for a restaurant, even if you're the head chef you're stuck with the restaurant menu and traditions and business policies."

"They don't let you try new recipes?" Cisco helped himself to a flaky buttermilk biscuit, too.

Gillian shrugged a slender shoulder. "Sometimes you get a little latitude. The owners will let you try a new dessert, or add a new entrée to the menu, but it gets very boring cooking the same list of things year after year. That's why I changed restaurant jobs frequently, early in my career, right along with Susannah, and later worked as an assistant for Susannah, when she became a restaurant consultant. She'd work with owners and regular clients to revamp the restaurant menus, I'd prepare the dishes and train the chefs on-premise to prepare the dishes exactly as Susannah wished."

Cisco understood always wanting to do more; it was the way he'd felt working side by side with Max. The bigger the challenge, the more he had enjoyed it.

Obviously, it was the same for Gillian. He was pleased they had that in common.

"How did Susannah talk you into coming out here with her?" he asked. Moving from California to Montana was a big change, especially for someone who had no family ties here.

Gillian smiled. "Susannah told me how beautiful Montana was. And that if I took the position at the logging camp kitchen, Max would give me carte blanche." Gillian smiled wistfully and a distant look came into her dark green eyes. "It wasn't a hard sell. I've always wanted my own kitchen to run as I see fit. And to have the run of several—well, that's a dream come true."

"The idea of being your own boss appeals to you," Cisco noted, aware that he, too, had the same take-charge, entrepreneurial spirit.

"In more than one way. I like being independent, Cisco." Gillian turned up her nose at him playfully. "Or hadn't you noticed?"

"Oh, I noticed all right," Cisco drawled. "It'd be hard not to." Just like he noticed the way the new denim split skirt and shirt, green cowgirl boots and flat-brimmed hat that she had changed into suited her.

"So when are you going to open the envelope Max gave you?" she asked softly, seeming now as curious about him as he had been about her.

Cisco looked down at his shirt pocket. He had been so busy trying to reunite Max and Pearl he had forgotten all about himself and what he had to gain in this cockeyed arrangement.

"I forgot all about that," Cisco murmured, already reaching for the envelope. Now that he thought about it, he did wonder what Max had given him.

He opened it while Gillian watched. Inside, as suspected, was a handwritten note from Max.

Cisco read it once, twice, hardly able to believe his eyes.

"Cisco, what is it?" Gillian demanded, leaning forward. She grabbed his arm and shook it lightly. "What does it say?"

Chapter Seven

"'Dear Son.'" Cisco read the letter from Max, his voice hoarse. "'I know you've felt a part of our family for years now, but you haven't officially or legally been part of the family. I want to remedy that, and this is one gift that has no strings attached. So herewith be advised that I have started formal proceedings—'" Cisco stopped as the enormity of what he was reading sank in, and he had to clear his throat before he could go on "'—to adopt you as my own son and give you the McKendrick name, to pass on to your own children, and have forevermore.'" Cisco swallowed hard around the lump in his throat. "'Remember, I love you. And will always be watching over you and yours. Max.'" Still shaken by the heartfelt generosity of Max's gift, but glad Gillian was there to share what had to be one of the best moments of his entire life, Cisco showed her the letter.

"Oh, Cisco." Gillian read it for herself, and handed it back. Her eyes shone as she scooted closer and wrapped her arms around him. "Congratulations," she murmured, hugging him. "This is so wonderful for you."

"Wonderful, and completely unexpected," Cisco said thickly, still feeling a little stunned as he folded the letter and carefully pocketed it. Though he'd felt like a member of the family for years, he'd never expected to actually be a McKendrick. He could hardly believe it was happening now.

"The McKendrick family mean a lot to you, don't they?" Gillian asked quietly as she gathered the lunch dishes and the food and put everything back in the picnic hamper with quick efficient motions of her slender hands. That done, she put her flat-brimmed hat aside and stretched out lengthwise on the blanket. Lying on her side, her elbow bent, her head propped on her hand, she continued studying him with an earnest, endearing manner.

Deciding to get more comfortable, too, he stretched out opposite her. "Patience, Trace and Cody have been like siblings to me. Max's been the father I never had but always wanted."

"Your mom was a single mother, then?"

Cisco nodded as he turned his eyes to the horizon. "I never knew my real father," he said quietly, hoping if he shared some of his innermost secrets with Gillian, she'd share hers with him. "He walked out on my mom and me before I was born."

Her green eyes shimmered with a depth of compassion that soothed. "I'm sorry," Gillian said softly, reaching out to cover his hand with hers. "It sounds like you had a really rotten time of it."

Cisco let himself savor the warmth and tenderness of her touch before he shrugged and met her eyes again. He had given up feeling sorry for himself years ago. "It's the way it was." Nothing could change it now. But something could change his relationship with Gillian, because she'd gotten to a place inside him no one else had ever touched. He realized he didn't want her to walk away and leave his heart empty again.

"What happened to your mom?" Gillian asked softly as she stroked the back of his hand with her fingertips.

"She died when I was eight, and I became a ward of the state." Cisco drifted back to that time of his life. "By that age, of course, I was considered too old to be adopted, and shunted from home to home." Some of the mountain of hurt he felt then crept into his voice. His lips curved in a rock-hard smile as he struggled to rein in the unwanted emotion. "I tried so hard to be whatever it was the foster parents wanted me to be. Good athlete? Okay, I'd do it. They wanted a class clown? Fine, I could do that. A brain? I could be that, too. And for a while, a short while, during what the social workers used to call the honeymoon period, everything would be right as rain. The foster parents would be so proud they'd been assigned such a good foster kid. And then it would happen." Cisco sighed and shook his head before he rolled onto his back, one hand propped behind his head, and continued in a low voice laced with regret. "Most of the time, I didn't even know what I did to get myself on the outs. I'd just know I'd be given the boot, and off I'd go to the next foster home."

Gillian's voice softened compassionately. "That must have been really devastating."

"It was." Knowing it would do no good to dwell on it, Cisco shrugged off the nights he'd cried himself to sleep, before he'd learned to toughen up and accept that was the way things always seemed to play out, no matter what he did. "After a while, I knew what was coming and I sped up the process. I tested 'em right off the bat to see what would happen. And just as quickly got tossed out and moved on to the next foster home." He paused, his low voice taking on a rueful edge. "Until it got to the point I had one foot out the door of a foster home before I even entered. By the time I was fourteen, I'd had enough of not belonging anywhere and I ran away. I ended up living on the streets of Butte, Montana, with other runaway teens," he recounted, some of the bleakness and despair he'd felt then creeping into his voice.

Her quiet understanding allowed him to go on.

"Unable to get a job because I was so young and had no phone or permanent address, not to mention a decent haircut, clothes or a bath, I learned to scavenge food from restaurant garbage bins and became adept at stealing, and that's how I survived for nearly two years." To his relief, Gillian did not look as horrified as he thought she might by his nefarious past. Instead, she seemed to understand and empathize with his plight to the point he was able to tell her the rest.

Where their hands were still linked, he entwined his fingers intimately with hers and recounted what had been the turning point in his young life. "One day, I picked Max's pocket. He caught me in the act and gave me a choice. Cops and jail, or one month of hard labor at his Silver Spur Ranch."

Gillian smiled. "That sounds like Max."

Cisco nodded. "You know it." Feeling restless, Cisco got up and sat back against the base of the tree that was providing their shade. Needing her close, Cisco took Gillian's hand and tugged her next to him. Seconds later, she was tucked in the shelter of his arm.

One hand curled around her waist, Cisco continued. "Fearing he'd throw me back to Social Services again, and another series of foster homes, or worse— a juvenile detention facility—I gave Max a made-up name, Cisco Kidd, like the famous outlaw. And I opted for the stint on Max's ranch, thinking I'd go there but run away again the first chance I got. But something happened when I got out here." Cisco shot a glance toward the granite mountain, rising majestically beyond the flower-filled meadow. He shook his head, recalling all he'd felt at being confronted with such a place. "It was so beautiful and clean and safe. So I decided to stay, at least for a day or two."

"Still, it must have been quite an adjustment for

you," she ventured softly, laying her head against his shoulder.

Cisco nodded, recalling just how tough it had been as he stroked a hand down the wildly curling softness of her long auburn hair. "I was a real city kid, and I had a chip on my shoulder the size of a Montana boulder. But Max hung in there and took me under his wing." Cisco paused, remembering how much his life had changed for the better then—almost as much—and as fast—as it was changing now with Gillian in his life.

He shifted Gillian, so she was sitting on his lap. "Before I knew it, Max had quietly gotten foster guardianship of me from the state and helped me legally keep the new name I'd facetiously chosen for myself and had come to like. He taught me the basics of ranching, logging and business, so if I ever left again I'd have job skills that would enable me to earn a living, and then he talked me into getting my GED. Once I'd accomplished that, and it didn't take very long with Max, Patience, Trace and Cody all tutoring me, Max dared me to try college and law school."

Cisco grinned, recalling the satisfaction he'd felt as he met goal after goal. "Again, with the help and support of the McKendricks, I succeeded. When I graduated and passed the bar exam, Max set me up in private practice and trusted me with his legal affairs. Since then I've tried hard to follow Max's example and lend a helping hand to anyone in need," he said in conclusion, proud of the progress he'd made.

"Like me?" Gillian guessed.

Cisco grew very still. "I admit my own experience left me with a sixth sense," he said, tightening his arm around her. "Having been there myself, I can just look at someone and know if they're running from the law or whatever. When I see they are," he admitted frankly, "I try to help."

"I see."

Cisco could tell by the way she tensed and slid off his lap that she disapproved of what some referred to as his charity work. "It's not a bad thing, Gillian," he said gently.

Gillian's lips tightened and her green eyes shimmered with hurt. "I'm sure the many women you've helped would agree," she tossed back, referring no doubt to a comment Pearl had made at the wedding reception.

Her slender shoulders stiffening, Gillian continued. "Considering the fact you took me in and married me—a person who undoubtedly has her own mysterious or nefarious past—Max must be very happy. After all, by taking me in and taking an interest in me, you're following directly in his footsteps, aren't you?"

Cisco heard the raw, humiliated note in her voice and damned himself for it. His lips tightened in frustration as he tried to explain. "Max doesn't control my life, Gillian—"

"But..."

"You're right to think he'd be pleased to know how close we've become." Because like it or not, Cisco admitted to himself, this was what Max had wanted for them.

CISCO'S ACKNOWLEDGMENT shouldn't have hurt her, but it did. It shouldn't have angered her, Gillian thought, but it did. She had wanted him to deny her softly voiced supposition. Tell her he was his own man. That he made his own decisions, and that he was as independent at heart and in spirit as she was. She wanted him to tell her he hadn't married her or made love to her because he was trying to repay some cosmic debt or felt sorry for her or had been trying to help her out of a jam. She wanted him to say he had married her because he had been as drawn to her as she was to him.

Instead, Cisco had calmly acknowledged he had gone the extra mile in order to both help her and follow Max's example as an exemplary humanitarian. Which led her to the next question. Had Cisco really made love to her last night because he had wanted her as desperately and completely as she wanted him? Or because it was expected of him, because "McKendrick men" were not only as wild and untamed as the Montana land they owned, but were expected to be white knights who were gallant, and sexy, and ultraprotective/possessive of the women in their lives?

She hated to think Cisco had reached out to her as

a way of proving his mettle to Max and keeping up with the other McKendrick men. But she had to acknowledge, given the wild courtships and marriages of Cody, Patience and Trace McKendrick, that it *was* a possibility.

Gillian sighed, upset.

Maybe she would be better off treating this partnership as a business opportunity that would challenge her professionally and ensure her financial wellbeing for the rest of her life—as she'd originally intended—instead of regarding Cisco as a man who would love her the rest of her life. Because to do otherwise, Gillian mused as Max's Silver Spur Ranch pickup truck abruptly came roaring through the trees, meant she would only get hurt.

"YOU'RE MISTAKEN," Max said, short minutes later, after he'd met up with them and returned the car distributor cap to Cisco so the couple could finally get out of there. "I know my woman and Pearl does not want to get married!"

Gillian rolled her eyes in exasperation. "Maybe because she feels you betrayed her," she said.

Max tipped his Stetson back on his head. "Well, she knows the kind of man I am. Hell—I'd never hurt her intentionally."

"You don't have to tell us," Cisco said.

"Well, heck, if I'd known this was gonna happen I woulda stayed married to her years ago!" Max exclaimed.

"Wait a minute!" Cisco interrupted, stunned. "The two of you were married! Where?" he demanded when Max nodded sheepishly. "When?"

"We got hitched in Las Vegas twenty-five years ago, but it was just for a day or so. Then she got mad at me and gave me the boot. We divorced and I returned to Montana."

"Then how did the two of you get together?" Gillian asked. Max and Pearl's lifelong love affair was legendary around these parts.

Max's wily blue eyes sparkled roguishly. "Let's just say she forgave me, moved out here and opened her diner with the help of a little business loan from me, and we've been together ever since."

"And the subject of marriage never came up again?" Gillian asked.

Max shrugged a buckskin-clad shoulder. "She made it very clear she'd rather be my lady friend instead of my wife. And that was fine by me, just as long as it made her happy. But now... Well, I wanted to see my kin settled before I proposed to Pearl."

"Apparently," Cisco said, trying to lighten the tone of the conversation.

Max grinned. "Guess I better do something about wooing Pearl right quick then, wouldn't you say? Meantime—" Max pointed at Gillian and Cisco "—long as you two lovebirds are finished meddling in my life, you two need to mosey on out to the honeymoon cottage."

"We're on our way." Cisco started toward his car,

distributor cap in hand, then stopped, remembering Max's gift to him. He wanted to say all that was in his heart, but he wasn't sure he could find words that would express even half of what he felt. "About the adoption—" Cisco lifted his eyes to Max's, and finished hoarsely "—it means the world to me."

"I know, son." Max beamed at Cisco like a father, and engulfed him in a warm, decidedly paternal hug. "Before you know it," Max promised, just as thickly, giving them both a cocky smile, "we're all gonna be one big happy family."

CISCO WAS STILL HOPING that was the case short minutes later as he parked his car in front of the honeymoon cottage.

"Oh my gosh, it's beautiful," Gillian whispered, surveying Max's gift to them.

"Isn't it," Cisco agreed.

The two-story log cabin with its steeply pitched gabled roof and wraparound front porch with a waist-high railing dated back half a century but until recently had gone unlived in. Max had not only had the place refurbished, Cisco noted, pleased, but he had added homey touches to the porch, such as high-backed pine green rocking chairs, rough-hewn tables and planters filled with flowers. It was going to be a great place to spend the next day and a half—and maybe even longer.

He got out of the car and went around to her side. Gillian—who still looked a little piqued at him—had already gotten out unaided so he contented himself with escorting her into the cottage.

Gillian's eyes widened in delight as she took in the high-beamed ceiling of the spacious living room. Red woven rugs added a touch of color to the gleaming hardwood floors. The leather sofa and sturdy wing chairs in blue-and-white plaid formed a conversation area in front of the fieldstone fireplace.

More compelling still, Cisco noted, was a framed photograph of them taken at the wedding, at the conclusion of the ceremony, just after he had kissed her. Gillian was staring up at him, starry-eyed. He, too, looked both lovestruck and dazed by the intensity of the passion between them. Gillian shook her head at the photo as she traced the sterling-silver edge of the frame with her fingertip and quipped, tongue in cheek, "If I didn't know better, I'd think we were in love."

"Which is, no doubt, exactly why Max left the photo here for us," Cisco drawled, knowing exactly how Max's mind worked. "To remind us that there are other reasons, besides property and wealth, why we should stay married." The same reasons, he thought, now causing havoc in his lower half.

Gillian read the sensual nature of his thoughts and rolled her eyes. "Good thing you and I are both too smart to be driven by our hormones indefinitely," she said wryly as she breezed on into the kitchen.

Were they? Cisco wondered, as Gillian studied their inheritance with a feminine eye. Blue-and-white gingham curtains decorated the many windows while a second fieldstone fireplace and built-in desk ran the length of an entire wall. She studied the mix of open shelves and cabinets on either side of the white, antique enameled stove. A food prep station commanded the center of the large country kitchen. Blue plaid rugs added a splash of color to the wood floor, while the vaulted ceiling added an aura of spaciousness.

Cisco did not need to be a rocket scientist to realize how much she loved what Max had done with this place, or know how much he could come to love it, too, with very little effort. His days as a bachelor had been lonely and empty, though he'd never realized it until now. Gillian had brought a sunny excitement to his life he knew he'd find very difficult to live without should this marriage not work out and they go their separate ways once their forty-eight hours together were up. Which was why he should give their relationship his all now, to ensure that didn't happen.

"As long as we're going to be sharing quarters, maybe we should work up some kind of schedule to make things a little easier," Cisco suggested, stepping closer. He was ready and willing to do whatever he could to make this arrangement work out for both of them, even past the forty-eight hours Max had stipulated. "You know, what time we get up in the morning, who cooks what and when, when we take our remaining two time-outs and so on."

Gillian quirked a decidedly uncooperative brow at

him. "How lawyerly of you," she murmured as she surveyed the view.

"Does that mean you disagree?"

"It means I don't want to be scheduled like just another charity function in your appointment book, Cisco. Furthermore, if you want to know the truth, I don't think that we need any more rules and regulations than are already set out in Max's deal with us."

So, she was still irked because she thought—erroneously, as it happened—he had only become involved with her because he was trying to return some of the generosity Max had bestowed on him.

Cisco studied Gillian intently, letting her know with a glance this was definitely not the case, as he reminded her quietly, "Max didn't specify very much."

Gillian quirked a dissenting auburn brow and refused to accept the fact that Cisco had helped her because he wanted to help her, not as some sort of obligation.

"Max specified enough," she said flatly. She turned on her heel and led the way up the narrow staircase in the kitchen, located next to the back door, that led to the second floor.

Cisco followed, watching her reaction as she realized the master bedroom occupied the entire second floor. This room, too, had a vaulted ceiling and steeply pitched roof. A skylight above the bed added additional light while a pine queen-size bed, piled high with pillows and quilts, and perfect for making long, wild love beckoned from the center of the room. There were two chests—one for each of them—and a closet filled with expensive Western clothing in both their sizes.

Gillian picked up the framed photo on the night-stand. It was another picture of them from the wedding. Slow dancing this time. Gillian was looking up at him. He was looking down at her. Remembering how she had felt in his arms, it was all Cisco could do not to haul Gillian in his arms and kiss her again, until all her anger and resentment faded, and just the fast-growing love and affection between them remained.

"Max just won't give up, will he?" Gillian murmured pensively.

Cisco shrugged, not too shy to admit, "He probably is just sowing the seed—"

"For us to get horizontal again?" Gillian quipped, deliberately making light of their lovemaking the previous evening. She shook her head in exasperation. "Considering the complications that's already caused in our relationship, I don't think so."

Wanna bet? Cisco thought, knowing his desire for her hadn't diminished in the slightest, no matter how much Gillian preferred to hope it might've. Nor had hers for him, he was willing to bet.

Arms folded in front of him, he watched as Gillian carefully set the second photo back down in the exact position she'd found it and breezed past him in a drift of hyacinth perfume to examine the adjacent bathroom.

Like the rest of the cottage, it had undergone extensive renovation while at the same time losing none of its rustic charm. It featured an old-fashioned claw-footed tub big enough for two, twin sinks and a separate glassed-in shower stall.

As Cisco looked around, it was all too easy to imagine Gillian in this room, getting ready for bed at night, getting ready for work in the morning. It was all too easy for him to imagine being married to her indefinitely, and dancing with her and kissing her again. And he knew he was going to have a heck of a time keeping his hands—and his kisses—to himself until she gave him the signal her temper had cooled and it was okay.

Cisco lounged against the doorjamb as Gillian examined the hyacinth-scented toiletries and sterling silver brush and mirror set Max had laid out for her. "You know Max is right about one thing. Staying under the same roof, even for thirty-one more hours is going to be tricky." Unless they laid a few ground rules.

Gillian set the perfume down with a thud. "So we'll have to manage."

"How?" Cisco bit out.

"We'll keep busy," Gillian decided smoothly, apparently having picked up on the ardent direction of his thoughts. She replaced the perfume bottle and headed down the stairs again, to the kitchen, having finished roaming the upstairs. "Besides, the honeymoon cottage is bigger than your apartment."

Cisco followed her, back to the living room and out onto the porch. "Not all that much bigger than my apartment," he said. Worse, it was all so damn cozy and he might as well admit it—romantic. It was the perfect place for an assignation.

Gillian sank into a rocking chair and, forearms resting flat on the arms of the chair, tested it out. "I suppose we could draw a line down the middle," she said recklessly as she rocked back and forth. "We could divvy up the territory that way—with you taking the sofa downstairs tonight."

Cisco perched on the rail and folded his arms in front of him. He did not want Gillian putting up a fence around her once again. "There's only one bathroom," he pointed out, mocking her with insolent eyes. "We can hardly draw a line down that."

Gillian shrugged insouciantly and avoided his searching gaze. "No, but we can eat and bathe at different times."

"You're being a little ridiculous, aren't you?" Cisco queried dryly. Even though he knew her resistance was probably par for the course.

"Not in my opinion, no, I'm not," Gillian said firmly, vaulting out of the rocking chair as suddenly as she had settled in. She slapped both hands on her hips and went toe-to-toe with him. Her eyes, already hot, turned to emerald fire. "I want my space, Cisco. In fact, I want a lot more space than I had last night."

Cisco had thought Cody McKendrick was a loner! But this woman had more barriers around her—heart and soul—than a wild stallion. So much so that Max had been wrong to think this forty-eight-hour marriage would guarantee any real closeness between him and Gillian.

For Gillian to fall in love with him, Cisco mused, she was going to have to want to fall in love with him. And that was something easier said than done. 'Cause the way he figured it, Ms. Gillian Taylor did not want to fall in love with anyone.

Gillian went back into the cabin and began to look around. "What are you doing?" Cisco watched her bend high and low as she opened one closet door after another.

"I'm looking for the rest of my belongings. I was hoping Max would have had them moved out here. Ah, here they are." She brought out a single suitcase and a toiletries case.

Cisco blinked at the meager belongings. "That's it? That's all you brought to Montana?"

Gillian nodded as she carried both up the stairs toward the bedroom. "I told Susannah I'd take the job but I wasn't really sure I'd stay," she explained.

"So what'd you do with the rest of your stuff?"

Gillian shrugged uncaringly. "Nothing. It's still in California."

"Just in case you decide to go back," Cisco ascertained as he lounged against the bedroom wall.

She nodded.

Disappointment sliced through Cisco, even as he tried to figure out how to get her to open up to him a little more, because without her confidence in him, there wasn't much he could do to help her, long-term. He slid his hands in the back pockets of his jeans and rested his weight on the balls of his feet. "I could help you unpack," he offered.

"No, thanks," she said primly, putting her bags in one corner of the bedroom, stepping away from him as far as the space would allow. "I won't be staying at the cottage all that long, so I probably won't unpack all that much."

It was a struggle to keep from reaching for her again, from taking her in his arms and making love to her until she melted against him in surrender once again.

But Cisco sensed he had already pushed her about as far as she was willing to go. If he overplayed his hand at this point, he could lose her forever.

Cisco walked with Gillian into the kitchen, stood idly by while she checked out every cabinet and counter and appliance with the look of a child on Christmas morning.

Max had figured right once again, Cisco thought. Knowing how she loved to cook, they might have a chance of keeping Gillian around here after all.

And as long as she was here, he had a chance to win her heart—not just for the moment, but for all time.

"So what do you think?" he asked, still watching her peruse the home that would soon be theirs.

Gillian smiled and shook her head as she reached for a row of cookbooks on one of the shelves. "I have to hand it to Max. This kitchen is a chef's dream. In fact the whole cottage, the clothes, everything, is simply spectacular." Her lips curved ruefully as she met his eyes. "To tell you the truth, it makes me feel a little guilty, accepting all this from Max," she admitted softly, penitently. She held up a hand before he could interrupt. "For you it's different, of course. With your devotion to Max, the way you've attended to his every need, you've earned all this and more, I suspect. But as for me...I've done nothing to deserve all this...and I'm not sure I ever could."

Unless of course you loved someone as difficult to love as me, Cisco thought, which was no doubt what Max had been thinking.

Without warning, his cell phone began to ring. Cisco took the slim, still-ringing phone out of his pocket and went into the other room to answer it. He was surprised to hear Lynda, the California private investigator, on the other end. "What's up?" he asked matter-of-factly, hoping against reason she had only helpful information and nothing upsetting to offer him. Just enough information to get the ball rolling and spur Gillian to confide everything in him.

But once again, it wasn't to be.

"I think you'd better sit down, Cisco," Lynda said heavily. "I have some very sobering news for you."

While Cisco was busy on the phone in the other room, Gillian checked out the contents of the pantry and Sub-Zero refrigerator. Max had seen to it that they'd have a staggering and sumptuous array of fresh food to choose from. The wine racks were filled with an equally sophisticated selection of fine wines. No doubt about it. The cottage was beautiful, inside and out. It was everything she ever could have wanted in a home. But she would never live there with Cisco, she realized uncomfortably, not unless she told him the whole truth. And she could never tell him the whole truth. Not without putting him in danger, too.

Footsteps echoed on the pine floor, then stopped.

Gillian turned. Cisco stood in the portal, looking at her. And the accusing way he was peering at her made the hair on the back of her neck stand on end. She knew abruptly by the grim set to his lips and the betrayed gleam in his pewter gray eyes that the fairy-tale quality of their time together had come to an end. She swallowed around the knot of apprehension in her throat and took a calming breath but it did not help. "What's wrong?"

Cisco clenched his jaw and continued to stare at her with a combination of anger and hurt. "I'd have to say that's a funny question, coming from someone who died ten years ago."

As the impact of his low, furious words hit her, Gillian froze. Oh, God. She should have known Cisco would find this out. Should have figured. Cisco had not gotten where he was in this life without being thorough. Still, if there was any chance she could protect Cisco—and indeed all the McKendricks—by keeping them out of the mess that had become her life, she would.

"What are you talking about?" she asked, feigning innocence. There was a tug-of-war going on inside her, so fierce she was breathless from it.

His whole body simmering with suppressed tension, Cisco pushed away from the jamb abruptly. He was through playing games, through giving her the opportunity to come to him in her own time. "Your Social Security number. Your name. Everything about you."

His goodwill exhausted, he crossed the distance between them in two long strides and clasped her shoulders tightly. "It's a fraud, isn't it, Gillian?" he demanded, his gray eyes glimmering with hurt.

She winced at the pressure he was exerting but did not dare drop her eyes from his grim, pinning gaze. "I still don't—"

"Cut the bull!" He shook her slightly, then released her with an angry shove and paced a short distance away. "Ten years ago, you took and claimed a dead person's identity as your own. So who are you, Gillian Taylor?" he growled, stepping treacherously near her once again. "Who the hell are you?"

Chapter Eight

Gillian didn't stop to think. She turned and ran. Out the back door, down the steps, toward the meandering ribbon of the Silver River, but still she could not escape the nightmare that had become her life. The footsteps pounding behind her...the sound of furious male swearing echoed in her ears...the hot breath on her neck...the feel of Cisco's arms around her as he caught her around the waist and forced her to face him. Suddenly it was all so terrifyingly familiar, and all so much more than she could bear. She cringed at his touch, forgetting for a moment that it was Cisco, and not the man who had dominated her nightmares for years, coming after her. "Don't," she moaned, putting both hands up to shield her face. "Oh God, don't hurt me!"

Her hysterical words ringing between them, Cisco let her go as suddenly as if she had burned him. His face was white with shock as he drew back. She had only to look up into the shocked contours of his handsome face to know he was devastated at the way she had reacted to his touch. And with good reason, she noted miserably, since he had never once done anything to harm her, since he wanted only to help. "Why would you think I would hurt you?" he asked softly. Hands jammed on his hips, he moved closer still.

Unable—unwilling—to answer, Gillian pushed past him as tears streamed down her face. Staring wordlessly at the mountains in the distance, she crossed her arms in front of her defiantly and brought them close. Heaven help her, she didn't want to get into this with anyone, least of all him. She wanted only to forget, but with Cisco staring her down, determined to sort things out, to help her find some level of serenity and safety at long last, that was not likely to happen, she knew.

"That cowardly bastard beat you, didn't he, Gillian?" Cisco guessed, his face tight with anger and distress as he stepped nearer still, not touching her, yet his warmth and his strength as tangible as his sandalwood and sage cologne. "Phillip didn't just stalk you, he beat you, and scared the hell out of you. And the police either couldn't or wouldn't do anything. That's why you took another identity ten years ago, isn't it?" he continued compassionately, his eyes softening with understanding as he let out a long anguished sigh. "That's why you've been running ever since, sleeping with a gun under your pillow. Why you've never become involved with another man." His hand curled with reassuring gentleness over her shoulder. "Because you've been scared to death and running for your life."

For a moment, Gillian let herself sink into the soothing reassurance of his touch. As much as she hated acquiescing to anyone, and staying here and talking this out with him against her wishes was acquiescing, she had to convince him to do things her way. She swung around to face him, knowing her face was strained and pale. "Please don't tell Max. Please don't tell Susannah. Don't tell anyone," she begged, all too willing to sacrifice her pride for the common good of everyone else on the ranch.

"Why not?" Cisco demanded, upset.

"Because I don't want them involved. I didn't want you involved, dammit." But he was, by virtue of his own incurable nosiness, and there was nothing she could do about it now. Thrusting her hands in the pockets of her split skirt, she ignored the ever darkening hue of his gray eyes, and shivering uncontrollably despite the heat of the midafternoon sun, she paced back and forth in the soft green grass. She wasn't as calm as she wanted to be, but she was still in control. "Don't you understand? I don't want anyone involved. It's too dangerous!"

"That's why you took on a false identity ten years ago," Cisco guessed, his expression strained.

Gillian nodded, knowing she had no choice now but to give him the whole truth, knowing even as she dreaded doing so that there was some relief in confessing all. She raked in an unsteady breath. "I realized faking my own death was the only way out. So I parked my car on a bridge one icy winter night and left a suicide note there, saying I just couldn't take Phillip's abuse anymore. I made it look as if I had taken a death leap into the Kansas River and then I disappeared.''

A pulse throbbing in his neck, he continued to study her. ''You have no regrets?''

''No, none,'' she replied softly, forcing herself to meet Cisco's sharply probing gaze, to take one step at a time, deal with it and move on. ''Phillip was never going to let me live, if I wasn't with him, and I couldn't be with him.'' She shrugged again, knowing on the one hand it all seemed like it had happened a lifetime ago, and in her dreams, like it was just yesterday. ''I knew what I had to do.''

Still struggling to take it all in, Cisco took her hand in his. For several minutes, as she worked to get a grip on herself, they walked along the edge of the meandering Silver River. Finally, his hand tightened over hers, imbuing her with the strength to go on. ''How did you get messed up with him in the first place?'' he asked compassionately.

If he only knew how many times she had asked herself that same question! Gillian felt tears blur her eyes as she brushed her pride aside. ''It's a long story.''

''I've got the time.'' Cisco paused and turned her so she was leaning against a tree. He brought her into the warm, strong circle of his arms and looked down at her with unbearable gentleness. "Besides, you've already told me this much," he said sympathetically. "You might as well tell me the rest."

Knowing he was right, Gillian released a weary breath, and aware he was waiting, forced herself to work through the misery and go on. "I was a freshman in college when my parents died, way too young and inexperienced to handle such grief alone, and I was devastated by their deaths. And that's when I met Phillip." She let out a little breath. "We were both students at KSU. He was ten years older than I was, and unlike anyone I'd ever met." She looked back, aware even now her memories of that time were a grief-filled blur. "It's hard to explain, but from the time we started dating, he just sort of took over."

Cisco caressed her cheek with his hand, understanding without her having to go into all the gory details, the way Phillip had systematically cut her off from all her friends. "When did the nightmare start?"

"About three months after we married," Gillian replied, taking a bracing gulp of air. She shuddered, remembering. "I was late coming home from the university library and he didn't believe that was the only place I'd been. He tried to get me to confess that I was running around on him, and I wouldn't, because it just wasn't true, and so he hit me to make me fess up. Later, when it was all over and he had calmed down, he cried and said it was the stress of grad school and living on a budget that was making him overreact like that." Ice gripped her heart as she thought about the flimsy reasons. "I told him that was no excuse. If he ever hit me again, I was leaving. The next time he did, which was three months down the line, I packed my bags and left."

"But that wasn't the end of it," Cisco guessed as he slid his hand down her arm until their hands were entwined.

Gillian shook her head grimly. She shuddered again, not understanding why she was suddenly so cold, just knowing she was. "The next day my car was vandalized while I was inside a shopping mall. He said he didn't do it, and the police had no proof, so they couldn't arrest him."

"I take it the harassment didn't stop there."

"No, it didn't." Unable to bear the pity she was sure was in his eyes, she looked at the horizon. "I managed to get a divorce over Phillip's protests, because I was so young and obviously grief-stricken and confused when we married, but the legal end of our marriage did nothing to convince Phillip our relationship was over. Over the course of the next year, Phillip broke into my apartment several times. He'd look through everything I owned, and leave just enough out of place so I'd know he had been there. When I tried to date someone else, the young man was mugged returning to his apartment late that night." Gillian shuddered. "He never saw his assailant. I was sure it was Phillip, but again, nothing could be proved.

"Meanwhile, Phillip kept sending me flowers and

candy and writing me notes that said I was the only woman for him, and he was the only man for me, and one day soon he would help me realize that." Gillian shook her head, aware neither the warmth of Cisco's body, so close to hers, or the sun beating down on them was enough to keep the chill away.

"I hired a lawyer to file harassment charges against Phillip, but his office was mysteriously broken into and he quit. I hired another. The same thing happened."

"Phillip," Cisco guessed.

"Unfortunately, I couldn't prove it. All I knew was that the attorneys were sufficiently intimidated to want nothing more to do with me or my case. And that's when I began planning my own death."

Cisco gently touched her face, his heart going out to her for all she had suffered. "You're still scared of him."

"Yes." Gillian hated that fact but knew it was true. "Very much." She leaned into the warm comfort of his touch and shook her head in frustration. "That's why I took on a false identity and lied about where I went to college, though I was scrupulously truthful about the type and amount of education I had. I didn't want anyone connecting me to Kansas, for fear it would trigger something in a computer somewhere and alert Phillip to the fact I was still alive."

Cisco paused. The rugged planes of his face softened in understanding. "You've never tried to find out what's happened to Phillip?" he asked.

Her heart pounding at just the thought, Gillian shook her head. She clung to him, trembling. "No. That's why I was so upset, seeing our photo in *USA Daily* on the Net. If Phillip sees that, and recognizes me—if he still wants revenge—he's going to know exactly where to find me."

His eyes still fastened firmly on hers, Cisco pointed out, "For all you know, Phillip could be dead now. For all you know, there's no longer any reason for you to be constantly looking over your shoulder or lying about your identity."

Gillian had never wished anyone dead, but oh, to be free again, to go through a day not having to look over her shoulder or worry her past would one day catch up with her again. She jammed her hands in the pockets of her denim skirt. "You're saying you could find out for me?"

Cisco nodded. He looked hard and dangerous. "Through Max's detective agency, yes."

"And Phillip would never know?" Gillian pressed, her heart pounding in her chest.

"He'd never have a clue."

Gillian wore a path in the grass on rubbery legs. "Suppose we do find him? Suppose he's still alive. Then what?" She worried anxiously, twisting her hands together and feeling sick with a combination of relief—that this might one day be completely over—and dread—that it never would be.

Cisco's lips curled in a dangerously feral smile.

"Then, depending on what we find, we decide what to do next."

"What do you mean, do?" Gillian demanded, for the first time fully aware—in her heart and her gut—of Cisco Kidd's streetfighter past.

"To set you free," Cisco explained, letting her know in a glance that if anyone knew how to effectively deal with her ex-husband, it was Cisco and indeed the whole McKendrick clan. Nevertheless, the fact remained that she knew what they were up against in Phillip; they did not. She folded her arms in front of her.

"I know you want to help, but I am not going back into that nightmare," she announced.

Cisco stepped closer, gave her a pitying look, then said quietly, "You've never left."

CISCO'S PROPHETIC WORDS still echoing in her ears, Gillian spun around on her heel and marched defiantly back to the cottage. She had known getting this close to anyone, never mind someone like Cisco, was a mistake, she thought as she charged up the stairs, tears streaming down her face. No matter what she did, no matter how far or how hard she ran, she could not escape her past.

"What are you doing?" Cisco's calm voice, seeming to come out of nowhere, made her jump.

"What does it look like I'm doing?" Ignoring her jittery state in the hopes that Cisco would, too, Gillian grabbed her suitcase and cosmetic case. "I'm doing what I should've done when Pete Lloyd thought I looked familiar. I'm getting out of here before anyone gets hurt on my account.''

Cisco remained in the doorway, rock-hard thighs girded, shoulders braced for battle, blocking the only exit out. ''You don't want to do that,'' he told her quietly, still looking as if he would defend her to the death.

Gillian ground her teeth on a hundred feisty replies. ''Don't tell me what I do or do not want to do,'' she announced with a haughty toss of her long auburn hair.

Cisco sighed but looked no less determined. He moved closer. ''Haven't you run from your past long enough?''

Gillian shook her head as tears of loss and longing blurred her eyes. Maybe it was unrealistic, but she had come to hope that they could work things out between them. Make this, if not a real marriage, a real romance, at least for a couple of wild and wonderful days. But that was not going to be, she realized sadly, and the truth was she had known that to be the case the moment she saw their photo in the Internet version of Monday's *USA Daily* newspaper. She just hadn't wanted to admit it to herself.

She held her ground and kept her distance. ''Get out of my way, Cisco.''

Ignoring her directive, he closed the distance between them, gently took her chin in hand and tilted her face up to his. They stood near enough that she could see the lines of strain on his face and the old hurts from his past in his eyes. And along with that the determination that their future would be better. "I'm not going to let anyone hurt you, Gillian," he told her, his expression hard, defiant. "Neither will Max or Trace or Cody or any of the men or women on the Silver Spur."

That said, he pulled her against him. Gillian buried her face in the warmth of his shirtfront and put her arms around him despite herself. "You can't protect me," she murmured, her voice muffled against the solid wall of his chest.

"Yes, I can, and I will." Cisco buried his face in the sweet-smelling softness of her hair. "In your heart, you know that," he whispered gently, tugging her even closer against his hard length. "That's why you're afraid." She gasped in surprise and wanting as his hands ghosted up and down her back. "Because it might mean you'd have to start taking risks again." His lips moved across her temple, down her cheek, to her lips, where they hovered over hers with tantalizing nearness and sent her heart slamming against her ribs. "It might mean," he said softly, looking deep into her eyes, "you'd have to stay.

"I know how hard this is for you, Gillian," Cisco said in a low husky voice that brooked no dissent as he lowered his head and kissed her with a rough possessiveness that stole her breath. "It was hard for me, too, when Max brought me here, but I gave it my all, and I've never regretted it. And that's what I'm asking you to do," he whispered.

"Oh, Cisco—" The sound of longing in her throat was cut off as his lips covered hers once again. His arm clamped around her back and he lifted her against him, and she had no choice but to feel the depth of his need for her. Or hers for him. She'd been running scared and alone for years. And now a strong, caring man had come into her life. It might not be wise, it might not be safe, but she couldn't resist the offer of a forty-eight-hour-long fantasy and marriage any more than she could resist Cisco's tender kiss.

Groaning with a mixture of despair—that this couldn't last—and exultation—that they'd found each other at all—Gillian returned his searing embrace with all her heart and soul. His hands moved to her breasts, cupping them through the fabric of her shirt. He parted her lips and slid his tongue into them, kissing her as if he had every right to do so, kissing her with a need that was deep and elemental and blatantly, unabashedly carnal. Melting into him helplessly, giving herself over as his wife, she took up the rhythm of his plundering lips and tongue, answering his hunger with a kiss that had him groaning, too.

He danced her backward, until he had trapped her against the wall and his body, and for that moment, there was nothing else between them—no promise of inheritance, no forty-eight-hour marriage—only this moment in time and the sweet, searing need. She wanted him. How she wanted him. And he wanted her, too.

His hands slid down the front of her shirt, unbuttoning as he went. His kiss grew wilder, more urgent, as he unclasped her bra and molded her breasts with his hands, drawing the nipples into pebble-hard tips. Her knees turned to putty. She melted against him, on fire and wanting...so much more....

"Cisco—" she whispered as another thrill swept through her.

"I know." He kissed his way from her temple to her shoulder, and pulled her against him, his legs on either side of her, his arousal pulsing between her thighs. "If I'm going to love you, we've got to get these clothes off."

Urgently they set about doing just that. Her body throbbing with unslaked need, they fell back on the queen-size bed, the sunlight spilling over them in a pool of soft golden light. Gillian had not seen how beautiful his body was the night before. She had only felt it, hot and hard and undeniably male. This afternoon she saw it. Reveled in it. The satin-smooth skin and muscle, and whorls of soft dark hair. Unable to help herself, she touched his flat male nipples. The sweat-slick skin of his chest and sinewy legs. She trembled at the intensity of her desire and the consequences it could bring. No longer caring, her hand moved lower still, to curve around him. He pressed against her, letting her know just what she did to him. She let her knees part. Her head fell back. She let her eyes shut.

Moving so she was beneath him, he took her nipple between his teeth and flicked it with his tongue. She gasped and arched off the bed and increased the caressing pressure of her hand.

Groaning, as if her touch were more than he could bear, he touched his lips to hers. Kissed her deeply, evocatively. He feathered soft, slow kisses along her hairline then slowly, ever so slowly and deliberately, kissed his way down her body. Pinning her hands on either side of her, he moved lower still. Her whole body was trembling with the need to take him inside her, but he wouldn't relent, not yet, not until she felt the searing stroke of his lips and tongue. She gasped as he found the feminine essence of her. And found it until it was all too much, until her heart was full and she shook with the force of her need. "Cisco, please. Let me…do…for you…what you're…"

He moved swiftly up her body. Lifting her with his hands, he brought her to him. "This is what I want," he whispered, staring down at her as he surged inside her.

Trusting as she had never trusted before, wanting as she had never wanted before, she gave herself over to sensation, over to him. This was a depth of feeling they didn't want and couldn't avoid. And as they moved together, surging up and over the edge, she knew it was a complication that was not likely to go away.

For long moments after, they lay locked together, breathing harshly in the silence of the room. "I'm not going to apologize for that," Cisco said finally.

"I don't want you to," Gillian murmured back,

burying her face in the solid warmth of his chest. For she knew better than anyone that there was no tomorrow, only today.

She had this moment, this man, this feeling of being protected and cared for and loved. And for the moment it had to be enough. Because it could all end tomorrow, she thought, waiting quietly for the reckoning to come.

Chapter Nine

"You all know I wouldn't have called this family meeting unless it were of paramount importance to all of us," Cisco began at four o'clock Sunday afternoon, as they gathered in his office. Aware how pale and nervous Gillian looked, he made sure everyone had coffee, then settled down beside Gillian and clasped her cold hand in his. He knew she had no desire to do this, just as he also knew it was absolutely necessary. Gillian had lived a life of terror long enough; working together, he and the McKendricks would help end her nightmare once and for all.

"We know that, son," Max reassured gravely, as he rested his Stetson on his buckskin-clad knee.

"What I don't get is why I was invited," Pearl interjected quietly as she passed around a plate of homemade Ranger cookies she'd brought over from the diner.

"Because you're as much a part of the McKendrick family as I am," Cisco told her gently.

"And you could be even more a part of it if you'd

just give me a chance to make things right with you,"
Max interjected emphatically, looking straight at
Pearl until she blushed.

"All right," Pearl said, still looking as if it was
going to be a very hard sell, convincing her of his
love. "I'll hear you out, Max." She glared at him
stonily as she settled on the opposite side of the room
from him. She folded her arms in front of her. "But
only after the family meeting has concluded."

Max nodded. It wasn't what he wanted, but it
would do. He turned to Cisco. "Back to the emergency that brought us here."

Briefly Cisco explained what Gillian had told him.
Everyone listened quietly. Not surprisingly, they were
all clearly as concerned for Gillian as he was. When
he had finished, Gillian broke in, looking more uncomfortable than ever. "I wanted to leave well
enough alone, rather than involve any of you in my
past."

Patience reacted as generously as Cisco had predicted she would. "Nonsense, Gillian. That's what
family is for," Patience said, settling into the curve
of Josh's arm.

"Patience is right. You should let us help you,"
Susannah said softly, taking her husband's hand in
hers.

Cody nodded and swept a hand through his long
wheat gold hair. "Take it from me, Gillian. I spent
seven years withdrawing from the world in the old
outpost, only to discover that all I'd done was take

my troubles with me and make them worse, in refusing to deal with them.''

Remembering the sweet, giving way Gillian's body had felt beneath his a few hours before, Cisco kept a firm clasp on Gillian's hand. "The only way out, the only way you will ever be able to have a full life, Gillian, is if you face this situation head-on and let us call in Sheriff Anderson.''

"The law can help you,'' Patience's husband, Josh, interjected quietly, putting his two cents in. "I know they'll do whatever it takes to keep you safe from harm, as will all of us.''

Gillian sighed. She plaited the fabric of her split skirt between her fingers and stared down at her knee. "I'm scared.''

Cisco heard the tears in her voice even before he saw them brimming in her eyes.

"I don't want anyone to be hurt on my account,'' Gillian finished on a husky whisper of soul-deep regret that only made Cisco's heart go out to her all the more.

"I felt the same way,'' Callie said softly as she wrapped her hand in Cody's. "But Sheriff Anderson and Cody helped me fight and win a years-long battle with my kin.'' Callie sent Gillian a reassuring look. "Because I stood up to them, I'm safe now. And you will be, too, if you let us all work together to help you.''

Gillian looked at Callie, then at Cisco, then the rest of the clan. As he had figured she would, when confronted with such love, warmth and understanding, she gave herself over to them. "All right, then," she said, forcing a tremulous smile, first at Cisco, then at everyone in the room. "Let's go for it."

"I TALKED TO PETE LLOYD," Cisco told the group assembled in Sheriff Anderson's office thirty minutes later.

"Did he recall how he knew me?" Gillian asked, aware she did feel safer with Cisco beside her.

Cisco put his arm around her and drew her in close to his side. "Not until I told him you'd been a student at Kansas State University, but had had to leave the state because of threats against your life. Then it all came back to him—your alleged suicide leap off the Kansas River bridge, and the suspected abuse at the hands of your ex-husband before that. Apparently, the local papers carried the story—and your photo—for weeks afterward."

Gillian rubbed the back of her neck anxiously, feeling as though the tension there would never leave, no matter what she did.

"What happened to her husband?" Callie asked.

His expression serious, a clipboard full of notes in his hand, Sheriff Anderson joined the family members gathered round. "That's what I need to tell you," he said quietly. "I just got off the phone with the Kansas police."

Gillian drew in a quavering breath and wished like hell she could get a grip. But that was something easier hoped for than accomplished. Just talking about her ex had brought back all the ugly memories with jarring force. "And?" she asked.

"Phillip Wingate's dead."

Gillian felt the blood drain from her face. She swayed, feeling as if she might faint, while everyone clamored at once.

"When?" Gillian demanded as Cisco tightened his grip on her protectively.

Sheriff Anderson looked as reluctant to be relaying the information as Gillian was to hear it. "He took his own life about a year after you were presumed dead."

Gillian paused and bit her lip. "That doesn't sound like him." And because it didn't, she found she had a hard time believing it.

Sheriff Anderson regarded Gillian solemnly. "Apparently your ex-husband was distraught by the note you left behind. For a long time he didn't believe you'd committed suicide. He made a real nuisance of himself looking for you and was arrested on disorderly conduct charges several times."

"How did the police react to that?" Cisco asked, reminding them all that in the ten years that had passed, law enforcement had taken a much tougher stance against domestic violence, and stalking laws had been changed and strengthened in many states.

"Although they couldn't prove anything, since Gillian—" the sheriff paused to consult his clipboard and correct himself "—or Meg Wingate's body was never found, they considered Phillip a suspect in his ex-wife's disappearance, as did many other people in the KSU community. Unable to live with the damage to his reputation, and the loss of his teaching assistantship at the graduate school—the university dismissed him when it all came out—Phillip Wingate drove to the same bridge where Gillian's car had been found, and took a suicide leap into the river. There were several witnesses that saw him jump, but as in your case, a body was never found to verify his death.''

"Which means—like me—he could still be alive,'' Gillian whispered as that information sank in, her nerves stretched tight on the razor's edge.

Sheriff Anderson and Cisco exchanged concerned looks with each other and the rest of the McKendrick men. "The police there admit it's possible, but they deem it highly unlikely that anyone, no matter how determined or strong a swimmer, could have survived a plunge into the river that night,'' Sheriff Anderson said finally. "The Kansas River was swollen from recent heavy rains, and the current was very fast. It's more likely that he drowned and his body was swiftly swept away.''

"I'm sorry, Gillian,'' Josh said softly.

"We all are,'' Cody agreed.

Trace nodded. "We wish you'd never had to go through that.''

"But now it's over,'' Callie concluded with heartfelt relief, taking Gillian's hand and squeezing it hard.

"And you're finally free to go on with the rest of your life," Susannah whispered joyfully as she and Patience embraced Gillian, too.

"All that's left to do is confirm the facts," Max said, "which we'll do immediately with the help of my crack private investigating team."

"And, of course, clear up a few legal matters after that," Cisco said.

Everyone seemed to think it really was over, Gillian noted as the grief and guilt she knew she ought to feel mysteriously continued to elude her.

But if that were truly the case, Gillian wondered uneasily, if her ex-husband was really no longer a threat to her, then why did she still have this sick, scared feeling in her heart?

"I'M SURE the dining hall is fine," Cisco insisted as they drove toward the logging camp a short while later. Gillian knew it was, too, but she had to be doing something to settle her nerves, and in the past, it was her work, her love of cooking, that had calmed her.

"I'll feel better if I check it and make sure there are no more raccoons taking up residence in the storeroom," Gillian said, trying her best not to let on how uneasy she still felt. Besides, the business was soon going to be hers, and she needed to show some responsibility so Max wouldn't think he'd make a mistake in willing it to her in the first place.

Cisco slanted her a concerned look. "You think the family of raccoons that tried to move in last night might have made an encore appearance?'' he asked with a look that said he knew exactly what she was worrying about.

Even though they were married, she didn't want him feeling anxious on her account. Gillian settled back in her comfortable leather seat. "It's possible, especially if their original home was destroyed in the storm we had the other night. Not to mention the fact the plastic we taped over the window was pretty flimsy. I'd hate to think of the chefs who will show up tomorrow being scared the way I was last night.''

The logging camp dining hall came into view. "Looks like we weren't the only ones with the idea to come here,'' Cisco said, noting the interior lights were on.

Realizing they weren't alone, Gillian's heart took on a slow, heavy beat.

"Is anyone supposed to be here?'' Cisco asked.

"No.''

His mouth tightened. "You wait here.'' He handed her his cell phone. "I'll check it out.''

"Cisco—''

Cisco reached past her, into the glove compartment and pulled out a small but lethal-looking handgun she had not realized he had. "Wait here,'' he repeated firmly.

Stopping only long enough to make sure his gun was loaded, he stepped out of the car. Gun held in front of him, he disappeared into the dining hall. Sweat pooled between Gillian's breasts and trickled down her rib cage as she held on to the cell phone so tightly, her hands ached. Was this what she had brought into Cisco's life? Fear? Uncertainty? Danger? And how could she allow it to continue, when he had been so good to her?

Seconds later, Cisco was back in the doorway, waving her in. "It's just Tom Turner," he told her in a confident, relaxed tone.

"I'm sorry I scared you, Gillian," the burly logging camp crew chief said as he, too, ushered her in. "I came by to check on the window that was broken out in the storm." His bearded face split into a worried frown. "And it's a good thing I did, too."

"Why? What happened?" Gillian asked as another prickle of unease slid down her spine. Maybe it was all the talk about Phillip earlier, but she couldn't shake the feeling something was amiss. "Was the plastic torn off the window?" By raccoons, or something—someone—else? she wondered nervously.

"No, it wasn't ripped off, but the whole bottom part had sort of worked loose. Packing tape doesn't usually do that. Generally it holds up pretty well, but I.guess in this instance the moisture from the storm must've affected it. Anyway, as you can see, I boarded up the opening with plywood until we can get the glass company out to replace the pane first thing tomorrow morning."

"Thank you."

"Did you see any evidence of raccoons?" Cisco

asked Tom, going on to explain they'd had some in the storeroom the previous evening.

"No, but I wasn't looking for any, either."

The three walked to the storeroom. To their mutual relief, all was in order—though only Gillian seemed to suspect that the plastic hadn't come off the window all on its own.

"Well," Tom said, "if you don't need me, I'll be going."

Gillian smiled. Some honeymoon this was turning out to be. Her life couldn't even stay calm for twenty-four hours. "Thanks for stopping by to check on things."

Tom smiled. "All a part of my job here." He tipped his head at her respectfully. "'Night."

"Good night," Cisco and Gillian replied.

After Tom left, Cisco turned to Gillian. He looked more than ready to call it a night. "Ready to go?"

Gillian nodded. Unless she found something to occupy her mind completely, it was going to be a very long night. "I just want to get a couple of my cookbooks. Susannah and I have been trying to perfect a recipe for low-cal manicotti, using ground chicken or turkey in the filling instead of ground beef—"

"Don't let Cody, the cattle rancher in the family, hear you say that!" Cisco interjected, as if she were speaking the ultimate heresy.

Gillian grinned and, ignoring his teasing, continued, "I'd like to study them tonight, and then if I have time tomorrow I want to experiment a bit in the kitchen.'' He abruptly looked so crestfallen, she wondered if he had made other plans for them he had yet to disclose. "You don't mind, do you?"

Cisco tugged her close and pressed a kiss to the top of her head. "Not as long as I get some attention from you tonight, too, and I get to taste whatever it is you cook up tomorrow.'' He wrapped his arms around her and fit her lower half to his, in a way that let her know he couldn't wait to get back to the honeymoon cottage so they could make love. As her heartbeat picked up, Gillian realized that she wanted that, too.

"It's a deal." Gillian smiled, reluctantly extricating herself from the warmth and tenderness of his protective embrace. She tilted her head back to his. "Anyway, it'll just take a minute for me to get what I need, so—''

"Go ahead." Cisco brushed his thumb across her lower lip. "I'll turn off the lights in the storeroom and lock up."

Both anxious to be out of there, they headed off in opposite directions. Let's see, Gillian thought, as she headed for her rack of cookbooks. She needed Volume III of the West Coast Publishing Series "Low-Cal Cooking" and the American Classics cookbook on "Italian Cuisine."

Her mind racing to the task ahead, Gillian reached for the books then stopped dead in her tracks. That was funny. Neither book was where it should be. She was certain she had arranged them in the right order the previous night. Once again, a chill slid down her spine and the hair on the back of her neck stood on end. What was going on here?

Without warning, Cisco appeared in the doorway to the dining hall office. He took a look at her face and the happiness faded from his silver eyes. He gazed into her face as if trying to see into her heart. "Everything okay?"

Gillian tore her eyes from his. This was ridiculous. She was panicking and overreacting, just as she had last night with the raccoons, and there was absolutely no reason for her to be behaving this way. There was not one hint, not one clue, that Phillip was still alive. In fact, everything they knew pointed to exactly the opposite conclusion.

Taking a deep breath, she decided she had to get a grip, for both their sakes. She stared at the shelf in front of her, to her chagrin still feeling embarrassed and off-kilter. "I'm having trouble locating the right cookbooks," she murmured, then just as quickly realized what had happened. "They're just a little mixed-up, that's all. Usually I put the general recipe books over here, the low-cal books down here, but it appears I've got them reversed. I guess I was distracted last night when I was reshelving them."

"You're sure that's all it is?" Cisco queried, stepping nearer.

Gillian nodded. She was not going to upset him.

"You look pale," Cisco continued.

She shrugged off his concern. "I'm just more tired

than I realized," she replied, knowing it was true, even if she didn't want to admit it. "It's been a long day." She tucked her arm in his. "Maybe we should get out of here?"

Cisco nodded. "Right away."

AN HOUR LATER, Gillian stood at the window of the honeymoon cottage. At long last, she and Cisco were alone again and, though she cherished the solitude, Gillian couldn't help but wonder—realistically speaking—if the next few hours were all the time they were ever going to have.

She wanted a real marriage with him more than she'd ever wanted anything in her life. The problem was, she didn't know what he wanted.

In the past twenty-four hours they'd already made love three times, and kissed more than that. But it wasn't enough, not nearly enough for her. And judging by the way Cisco kept touching her at the slightest excuse, and holding her close, it wasn't enough for him, either.

They hadn't mentioned love, either of them, though she knew in her heart that was what she felt for him. But what did he feel for her? Besides the need to rescue her? Or the yearning for a passionate affair?

She knew they were going to have to talk about it before this arrangement of theirs ended. She just wasn't sure she was ready to hear the answers.

Nor, as he drew the drapes in the living room and

made sure the cottage was locked up tight as a drum, did he look ready to give them.

"Okay, what gives?" Cisco asked finally. Taking her arm, he guided her to the long leather sofa, sat down first and pulled her onto his lap.

Gillian curled into him, as a fresh wave of fear, that their love was not strong enough to make it over the long haul, washed over her.

"I'm just edgy, that's all," she said, burying her face in Cisco's strong shoulder.

"About Phillip?"

And us. Especially us. What if he decided when all was done, all he had ever wanted from her was an affair? What then?

Gillian curled her hands around his waist, holding on for dear life even while the unspent adrenaline, still left over from the nagging suspicion someone had been at the dining hall, sifting through and rearranging her meager belongings, pulsed through her. She didn't want to be the only one who felt love in this relationship; it would hurt too much, if that were the case.

Needing Cisco more than ever, she cuddled closer and ran a hand over the solidness of his chest as she continued. "It's just hard for me to believe it's really over."

"I know what you mean. The resolution does seem almost too easy after all you went through the last ten years," Cisco commiserated gently, as he stroked a hand through her hair.

Gillian sighed and drew back to look at him, feeling stunned by the closeness, the intimacy, that had developed between them in so little time. If it wasn't love they felt—what was it?

"I just want to put the ugliness of the past behind me and get on with my life," she told him. *I want to have a real marriage to you.*

Cisco's gaze softened as he lifted her hand and pressed a light kiss across the back of her knuckles. "I want you to be able to forget the bad times, too," he said huskily.

Gillian released a shaky breath and then shivered as a chill, caused by her nervousness, came over her.

"In the meantime—" Cisco reached for the afghan on the back of the sofa and wrapped it around her shoulders and back "—you're safe here, Gillian," he told her, pulling the folded edges of the afghan together, using them to draw her closer to him as her pulse took on a heavier beat. "You'll always be safe with me," he said, and then he kissed her.

The need he generated was deep and aching and not to be denied. Desperate to forget the grief and trauma of the day, Gillian let herself fall into the kiss, let herself take pleasure in the feel of his lips on hers, his hands on her breasts, moving between her legs. When he unbuckled his belt and shucked his trousers, she shimmied out of her skirt and panties. Loving the look of pleasure and adoration on his face as she straddled his lap, she opened herself to him, needing to feel him inside her, needing to be as one. There was so little time. So much she wanted. So much she didn't know. But one thing was certain, she thought as she abandoned herself to the pleasure of their love-making. If the police were right and her nightmare had ended once and for all, then she was free now. Free to love again. Free to build a life. Free to walk down the street without fear. And that was something she wanted desperately to believe was hers. Something she wanted almost—almost—as much as she wanted, and why not say it, *loved* Cisco Kidd.

Cisco knew, even as he made her his, that this was, perhaps, the last thing they should be doing, given the shock Gillian had had earlier in the day. He couldn't help it. He was a man and she was a woman, and everything they had been through today, when combined with their need for each other and the passion sizzling between them, demanded they take this time for each other, shut out the rest of the world and just be together, as a husband and wife were meant to be.

He didn't know what tomorrow held, or the day after that, but for now, for tonight, he wanted to protect her, take away her pain, her past, and give Gillian this moment in time. He wanted to love her and make her his with every stroke of his hand, every thrust, every deep, searching kiss, every flame fueling the burning in his loins. He wanted to offer comfort and give her her future back, he wanted to ease her loneliness and his, and discover the possibilities of what could be, in this crazy spur-of-the-moment marriage of theirs.

And, as they clung together and her hips moved in perfect rhythm with his, and he absorbed the comfort of her soft warm body and she lost herself in him, he felt in some way he had.

She tangled her hands in his hair and whispered his name as her climax gripped her. And then it was too much. Her thighs burned against his, her whole body trembled and melted into his. He was caught in the grip of feeling so intense, he couldn't breathe. He surged into her, spilling his seed as the need flowed over them, bonding them together just as surely as the wanting.

His heart still pounding heavily in his chest, he held her close, their bodies shuddering. This, he thought tenderly, as she clung to him wordlessly, was what it was all about. Being close to someone. Wanting them as they want you. Sharing. The good times and the bad. The fears and the grief. The innermost secrets, dreams, hopes for the future.

Max had been right, Cisco thought, still holding her tight. They could have all that, and so much more if they just gave themselves—gave this marriage—a chance.

And that was when Cisco felt it; the dampness of her tears on his shoulders, soaking through his shirt.

Alarmed, he tucked a hand beneath her chin and lifted her face to his, knowing that tenderness and love was her undoing, just as it had once been his. Yet she needed his protection and tender loving care, even if she wouldn't quite admit it to herself. "Tell me what's wrong."

Gillian shook her head, looking as if she didn't trust herself to speak.

"Tell me," he commanded softly, with the pads of his thumbs wiping away the tears that continued to flow. Were they a simple result of the overabundance of adrenaline that had been running through her all afternoon, he wondered, knowing at heart he was an old-fashioned guy trying to deal with a woman who was as decidedly un-old-fashioned and independent as could be. Or were the tears caused by something more? Something she had yet to tell him. There was no deciphering the source of her conflicted state, given the guarded, vulnerable look on her face, the way he could already feel her drawing herself in, pulling away from him, the way she did whenever she seemed to think he was getting too close to whatever secrets she still held in her closely guarded heart.

Finally getting a grip and pulling herself together, Gillian drew a breath and looked away in embarrassment as she confided shakily, "I was just thinking this might be the very last time we're together, given the deal we made. But I want you to know something, Cisco." She rushed on, putting up a hand before he could interrupt. "My time with you has meant everything to me. Everything."

Cisco stiffened. Past experience had shown him that when people said reassuring things like that it was generally a prelude to their walking out the door on him and not looking back. No one had ever meant to hurt him, he thought as he, too, put aside his own vulnerability and desire and pulled himself together, but they had just the same. He just hadn't expected it from Gillian. Not now. Not this evening. But, Cisco thought, maybe this was what he got for pushing the envelope where their spur-of-the-moment marriage was concerned and making love to her that first night together.

"It's meant a lot to me, too," he replied gently, his deeply ingrained gallantry intact, even as the rest of him felt like a rodeo cowboy who'd been slammed to the ground by a bucking bronc.

"But..." she prodded, wrapping the afghan closer around her slender form.

Cisco sighed and rubbed at the tension in the back of his neck. Call him a damn coward if you want, call him just flat-out selfish, but if a kiss-off was coming, he didn't want it to happen until after the full forty-eight hours Max had alloted them were up.

Wordlessly he shot to his feet, swept her up into his arms and headed for the stairs. Whether she wanted to lean on him or not, she was going to do it, at least for the next twenty-four hours. And maybe even longer than that....

"What are you doing?" she gasped.

"We're going to bed. Under the terms of our agreement with Max, we've got one more night together," he told her determinedly as he carried her into the bedroom that was theirs, ever so gently lowered her onto the comfortable bed and draped her body with his. "And I for one don't intend to waste it."

Chapter Ten

Gillian woke to the smell of coffee and an empty place beside her in the bed. Drawing the rumpled covers around her nakedness, she sat up, pushing the hair from her eyes. It was still early, barely 7:00 a.m., but she wasn't surprised Cisco was up. They'd made love so often and so passionately that neither of them had slept much during the night. And though she'd been as simultaneously distracted and satiated by the ardent lovemaking and comforted by the act of holding each other as he had, she also knew whatever happened next was not going to be easy or painless, no matter what Cisco thought.

Because with Phillip's death still unsubstantiated, she couldn't see a future for them, not when the Internet's *USA Daily* article had made it clear she was still alive, and had given her location, not when she still worried it was possible that her mere presence on the Silver Spur Ranch could bring danger and trouble to those she loved.

That being the case, there was no point in prolonging the inevitable. No point in hurting each other any more than they had to hurt each other. And she knew now more than ever after last night that leaving Cisco was going to hurt.

The sound of a pickup truck rumbling up the drive sent Gillian to the window. Looking down, she saw Patience getting out of the cab, a wicker basket of what looked to be home-baked goodies over her arm. One of the Silver Spur cowboys was with her, which was odd, Gillian thought. Usually Patience tooled around the ranch on her own.

Figuring she might as well see what was going on, Gillian pulled on a robe and went into the bathroom to brush her teeth and splash some cold water on her face. She quickly fashioned her wildly curling auburn hair into some semblance of order, then found her slippers and headed toward the stairs. If Patience was here this early, she no doubt had a very good reason, Gillian thought, her heartbeat already picking up. And perhaps even some news....

"SO HOW'S SHE DOING?" Patience asked.

"Not good." With every second that passed, Gillian seemed to get further away from him in an emotional sense. It was as if she had resurrected all the barriers that had been between them from the get-go and then added a fire wall of resistance on top of that.

He understood her not *wanting* to involve him. He just couldn't stomach her pretending that he wasn't in this as hip deep as she was, when they both knew, because of his growing feelings for her, that was exactly the case!

"Does she know Max had guards stationed around the cottage last night?"

Cisco's glance cut to the framed photo of them taken at the wedding. The one taken right after he had slipped the ring on her finger, and at Max's playful urging, indulged in that reckless, but oh-so-pleasurable first kiss with her. One only had to look at the photo to see how magical their relationship had been, even then. Which led him to wonder, how could everything have gone so right and so wrong in such a short space of time?

"No, I didn't tell her. I didn't want to worry her."

"But you think there's a chance—however remote—that her ex-husband is out there, too, don't you?"

"I'm hoping against it, but I think, until we know for sure, that we ought to stay prepared for anything," Cisco said grimly.

"I agree. Which is why we all sort of got together and agreed this is not the time for *Personalities!* magazine to do an in-depth profile on Max and the family."

Cisco frowned. "I didn't know that was in the works."

"The managing editor just got in touch with Max yesterday—before the family meeting. Apparently, the magazine had been planning to publish a commemorative piece on him, as one of the last truly powerful men of the Old West, along with his obit.

Then they saw the *USA Daily* article on the Internet Sunday morning just before it got pulled, and learned Max was alive, and had cooked up the unusual way of giving us our inheritances as a way of getting us back together with our true loves. At that point the magazine became—as you can guess—even more interested. And, if the situation had been different, Max and the rest of us probably would've done it. You know how proud Max is of his accomplishments and ours, not to mention the McKendrick family as a whole.''

"Yeah," Cisco agreed, knowing it must've disappointed Max to have to turn this down. "It would've been quite a coup for him."

"Which, in this case, is neither here nor there, because Max doesn't want to do it unless you—and Gillian, too, of course—are included in the profile, too. He wants everyone to know of his plans to adopt you—"

"Then just wait a day," Gillian interrupted coolly, "and it won't be a problem."

Cisco and Patience turned simultaneously. Gillian lounged in the doorway to the kitchen. It wasn't too hard to figure out from her miserable, distracted expression that she was still struggling with her guilt at having brought her troubles with her to the ranch.

"After all, by then, we'll both have inherited, our marriage will be over and you can do the article without ever making mention of me."

Patience flushed. "I think you misunderstood. We

don't want you to leave. For heaven's sake, everyone in the family adores you!''

"Everyone's been very kind, but that's not really the point, is it? My marriage to Cisco was a sham from the get-go, and while it's been…interesting, it's not the real thing."

Cisco wanted more than anything to comfort Gillian, even as he saw—as part of the punishment she was determined to inflict upon herself—that she was not going to allow it.

"You can't mean that," Patience declared. "I mean, I saw the two of you together yesterday at the sheriff's office. I saw how you were leaning on him."

"Right. I needed a lawyer and a friend and Cisco was both. But now that's over, too. And since it is, we need to move on."

Cisco looked at Patience. "Thanks for stopping by, but if you don't mind, Gillian and I need some time alone."

"No problem. I'll show myself out." Which she did in silence.

"It's not about that, is it?" Cisco asked Gillian.

Color came flooding back into her cheeks as Gillian's breath hitched in her throat. Though she hazarded a glance in his general direction, she couldn't quite meet his eyes. "I'm not saying we're not good together in bed. We are," she admitted hoarsely. "And that's the problem. There's been too much of that the last two days."

Conceding to her obvious wishes, Cisco physically kept his distance, for the moment anyway. He lounged against the counter, fastening a hand on either side of him. "I admit everything happened too fast," he said carefully, still keeping his gaze trained on her face.

But as for the rest, he had never before been wanted—the way Gillian had seemed to want him— or needed.... When he was with Gillian, he'd gone from being on the fringes, on the outside looking in, to being part of the McKendricks.

Gillian's glance cut to the sterling silver picture frame on the table. She studied the photo of them, too. The depth of her longing to return to that much safer, simpler time in their two-day relationship was apparent as she raked both her hands through the ends of her wildly curling hair, then vaulted to her feet.

"The point is," Gillian said wearily at last, "it shouldn't have happened at all because it clouded things, Cisco."

Cisco knew she was acting out of bravado, trying to get her inner toughness and tenacity back. And while he understood that her actions made sense—at least to her—in the short run, they didn't make sense in the long run. Particularly considering all they could have, if they just stuck it out and stuck together.

It was, however, predictable that she was now feeling this way because Gillian and he were alike in that regard—they were used to living a solitary life.

Which was, Cisco thought, yet another reason why Max had stuck them together the way he had, so neither of them could run.

"The lovemaking made us lose sight of the end goal," Gillian continued seriously.

"And that was…?"

"My inheritance. Yours." Briefly, guilt crossed her face. Then her soft green eyes became steady and earnest. "You earned your gift from Max, with years of devotion and hard work," she explained matter-of-factly, "but mine was a free ride, and one I intended to enjoy. The giddiness I felt over the prospect of my windfall, coupled with my boredom at being stuck out here alone with you, with nothing to do…but be together, carried over into my relationship with you." She stopped and shook her head ruefully. Cisco could imagine all she was regretting: the kisses, the confessions, the breath-robbing intimacy of their time together. They were so close…and yet suddenly so far apart—farther than ever…. His stomach twisted around itself, like a clenching fist. "So what are you saying?" he demanded, wordlessly pleading for her not to say the words he sensed were coming.

Gillian smiled at him. "We need to step back from each other and clear our heads now that the end of our forty-eight hours together is approaching."

"Meaning what exactly?" Cisco queried, surprised the betrayal could leave him feeling so winded and utterly dejected. Hadn't common sense told him this was coming from the onset? He regarded her steadily, realizing with crushing disappointment that his romance was not going to turn out anywhere near as successfully as those of the other McKendrick heirs. Which was, he supposed, another reason why it had taken Max so long to take steps to formally include him in the family. Because Max knew damn well that it took more than court documents or the fact he had really grown up here under Max's tutelage, and become a man on this ranch, or been an unofficial son to Max and "brother" to Cody, Patience and Trace to make someone a real McKendrick. Because a real McKendrick would never have let a woman like Gillian slip away from him.

Gillian sank down in one of the upholstered chairs in the living room. "Now that my life has more or less been sorted out and I'm free of my past, my need for protection is gone. You can turn your energies to helping someone else."

"Helping them."

"Yes."

"Just like that."

"It happened fast for us. It can happen fast with someone else. It's for the best."

Cisco rubbed at the knots of tension in the back of his neck, aware he had never felt so disillusioned in his life, even as he forced himself to pin Gillian down on her intentions. "So, in other words, you're ditching me and our marriage as soon as possible?"

Gillian shrugged. "We have to face facts. This was a great fling for both of us, no doubt about it. But, for a lot of reasons, that's all it was or ever will be. That being the case, we need to thank Max for the opportunity to know each other, assure him that yes, indeed, there were plenty of sparks, just as he thought, but also tell him, despite his best intentions, it's not going to work, and go our separate ways."

She sounded as though she had it all figured out, Cisco thought angrily. And though his first impulse was to simply say to heck with it, to heck with her, he forced himself to stay there with her. To do what Max had advised and listen to his heart, which was telling him to stay.

Wanting something is half the battle, Max had said. *Working for it, despite the often-powerful adversities you encounter, is the other half. So when you find happiness…you need to forget your fears, forget all the reasons why you think this…won't work and reach out with both hands and grab the happiness that's waiting for you.*

Knowing Max was right, that he couldn't just let Gillian go without a fight, Cisco regarded Gillian and tried again to reach her to make her see that even though they had only been together a short time, they had too much, far too much, to simply give up on each other. "I know you're upset," he began. In fact, he imagined she was as emotionally worn out by all this as he was.

"That's just it. I'm not," Gillian said, a stubborn light coming into her guileless green eyes. "This business with Phillip has made me think clearly again. It's helped me know what I have to do."

"And that is?" Cisco asked.

"Do everything I can to help secure your inheritance, and then go my separate way as soon as the forty-eight hours are up."

CISCO DIDN'T AGREE with her, but it didn't matter. Gillian waited until Cisco was in the shower, then left the honeymoon cottage via the back door. Her purse slung over her shoulder, she headed briskly down the back steps. She had to do the right thing, not just for the both of them, but for all the McKendricks, even if it broke her heart—and Cisco's, too. Heaven knew she had never meant to hurt him, she thought with a wellspring of regret. But the simple truth of the matter was that she had just by drawing him into the hell that had become her life, and now she had no choice but to do what she was doing.

Cisco needed someone who would stay. Someone he could count on to be there for him through thick and thin. Someone who wouldn't bring heartache and trouble into his life. He needed someone who had no scars, no troubled past.

As much as she was loathe to admit it, it wasn't going to be her, Gillian thought. He had to know it from the outset, too; he was just too stubborn, too eager to please Max and become a real McKendrick, to admit it.

To protect him, she'd had to be cruel, and quick. He didn't understand now. Maybe later he would. And even if he didn't, she told herself firmly, it didn't matter, because once she was away from the ranch, he would be safe.

"Hey, Gillian, everything okay?" the cowboy standing guard over the back entrance asked.

Gillian nodded and paused. "What are you doing here?" she asked curiously, stunned to see anyone else there, too. After all, the whole point in bunking her and Cisco at the honeymoon cottage had been to give them privacy.

The cowboy shrugged a little uneasily. "I'm standing guard."

So, Gillian thought, others shared her suspicions, too. They just hadn't thought enough to let her in on that. "Cisco ask you to do that?" she inquired, as if it were no big deal even if he had.

The cowboy nodded laconically. "And Max." He looked at the purse she had slung over her shoulder. His eyes narrowed. "What's up?"

Gillian prayed that someday Cisco would forgive her for the duplicity. "I've got to go over to the dining hall to see about getting new glass put in the office window that was damaged by the storm," she fibbed.

The cowboy tipped his hat back. "You're going by yourself?" he asked in a wary tone meant not to alarm her.

"Yes."

The cowboy frowned and looked all the more uneasy about what she was proposing to do. "I thought you and Cisco were supposed to stick together," the young cowboy reminded her.

Gillian forced a casual smile. "Under the terms Max stipulated, Cisco and I have a time-out coming. Two, as a matter of fact. He's going to meet me there in thirty minutes."

The cowboy followed Gillian to Cisco's car and

held the door for her as she climbed in. "You want me to ride over with you?"

"No, Cisco needs you here," Gillian lied, fitting Cisco's key in the ignition. "Really, I'll be fine."

"Well, you be careful now," the cowboy continued. "This is a big ranch. You never know what kind of trouble you might happen upon."

Actually, Gillian knew the ranch was the one place Phillip wasn't. Phillip just wanted her to think that was where he was hiding out. She'd bet anything he had hitched a ride and was already back in town. Looking for ways to hurt her and Cisco, even as the moments ticked out. Situating himself in the one place he knew Cisco and perhaps even *she* would eventually show up.

CISCO DID A CURSORY SWEEP of the first floor, then scowled at the kitchen counter, noting his keys were not there, either. "Damn it all to hell, I cannot believe she did this to me!" he muttered as he stormed out the kitchen door. "Where's Gillian? Where's my car?" Cisco demanded to the cowboy standing guard.

While Cisco's blood boiled, the cowboy dutifully repeated what Gillian had told him.

Cisco swore again, and the cowboy began to look edgy. He narrowed his eyes at Cisco. "Does this mean you didn't want her to go over to the dining hall alone?" he asked.

"That is exactly what it means," Cisco replied through set teeth, doing his best to take his latest disappointment in stride. "When did she leave?"

The cowboy glanced at his watch, the red flush in his neck climbing into his ears. "Five minutes ago. Maybe ten."

That was way too much of a head start for a woman as accomplished at being on the run as Gillian. "Get on the shortwave," he commanded the cowboy tersely, doing his best to think levelly—not easy, when the woman he loved was in danger. "Send out a blanket message to all the hands, asking where my car and Gillian Taylor were last seen."

The bowlegged cowboy swiftly strode over to his Silver Spur Ranch pickup truck and did as ordered. Several replies later, he had the answer Cisco had been waiting for.

GILLIAN PARKED in front of the converted stables that housed Cisco's Fort Benton law office and the loft apartment where he lived. She cut the motor on his luxurious sports car with a trembling hand. The blinds were shut, just as they should be, for a law office that would be closed for the next two weeks. Two weeks Max had intended for their honeymoon.

Glad no one else was there, no innocent bystander to get hurt, Gillian took the keys from the ignition, picked up her purse and stepped out of the car. Aware the offices down the block had emptied out for the noon lunch hour, she walked up the sidewalk and stepped onto the covered porch, pausing in front of the heavy oak door with the engraved gold-plated sign that read Cisco Kidd, Attorney-At-Law.

Wondering if she would ever see that—or him—

again, yet knowing she would still do anything she had to do to protect the man she loved with all her heart and soul, Gillian unlocked the door with Cisco's keys, and headed inside.

Her heart slamming against her ribs, Gillian walked through the door of the luxuriously appointed reception area and into the adjacent law library that had been Max's gift to Cisco upon his graduation from law school. It was neat as a pin, and just as Cisco had left it. Knowing her ex-husband's vicious temper, Gillian had half expected this all to be destroyed by now. The fact it wasn't gave her hope.

Maybe Phillip wasn't here after all, she thought on a relieved sigh.

Nevertheless, every sense attuned and alert, she moved cautiously into the secretary's office, where all the typing and copying and clerical work were done. Again, to her mixed feelings of suspicion and relief, everything seemed to be in order. Taking a deep breath, she pushed open the closed door to Cisco's private office. Standing calmly behind Cisco's desk was the demon from her dreams.

Chapter Eleven

"You're looking good, Meg," Phillip began.

And he hadn't changed, Gillian thought. He was still the same wolf in sheep's clothing she had been duped into marrying years ago. The difference was she was not the same innocent young woman, lost and alone, and reeling with grief.

"Phillip," Gillian whispered hoarsely as her heart began to pound.

Even as she spoke, she wondered how her ex-husband did it—managed to look like any urban professional, off on a weekend jaunt—when underneath he was so cold and so cruel. Maybe it was the black Polo shirt, khaki Dockers slacks, and loafers. Maybe it was the black hair, so neatly cut and combed, the handsome suntanned face, and dark brown...almost black...eyes. The outgoing demeanor and casual, sauntering walk. All she knew was that at six foot two inches tall and some 180 pounds Phillip would win any physical contest between them hands down.

Therefore, she had to buy time, gauge his immediate intentions, and outsmart him!

"I thought you were dead," she said, and saw a flicker of cold amusement in his black eyes, before the grim anger and cold, civil smile returned.

"That's not surprising. After the stunt you pulled, I had *no choice* but to put on a wet suit that would withstand the freezing cold river, leap from that bridge, and fake my own death. With everyone I knew—not to mention the police—suspecting me of foul play in your demise—" Phillip shrugged his shoulders uncaringly even as his eyes narrowed and his lower lip curled resentfully. "You can imagine how tough it would've been for me to get a decent job with that suspicion haunting me. So I created a new identity, moved to Dallas where no one would recognize me, and took an investment banking job there."

"Obviously, you've been successful," Gillian noted. Just as she knew he always would be.

Phillip shrugged and kept his eyes on hers. "Professionally and financially, yes, I have been. Personally is another matter," he admitted as his eyes burned with a strange, passionate light. "My darling Meg. I told you that no divorce would ever ruin what we have and I was right," he finished with something akin to amazement. "To this day, no woman has ever been able to take your place. In fact," he told her wistfully as his hands tightened into fists and he flashed her an odd, contented smile, "not a day went by that I didn't dream about what I'd do if I ever found you again.''

Oh, God, Gillian thought as her legs began to shake. I was right. Even after all this time, nothing has changed. He's still as nuts, and obsessed with me, as he ever was.

''So you can imagine my surprise Saturday evening—when I returned home from a date with yet another woman who could not begin to compare with you—' Anger suddenly lit Phillip's eyes. His lips tightened in a grim parody of a smile as he raked her with a hot glance and continued to reflect, ''There I was, thumbing through the Internet edition of *USA Daily,* looking for the latest financial news, when what should I see but your picture.'' He shook his head, clearly savoring that moment every bit as much as Gillian had always dreaded it. ''I have to tell you, Meg,'' he whispered seductively, as a muscle worked angrily in his jaw. ''Finding you again after all these years was like a dream come true.''

A chill went down Gillian's spine at the possessiveness in his low voice, and the twisted love in his eyes.

''So I hopped on the first flight out yesterday morning, rented a car at the airport in Helena, and drove out here to investigate the situation for myself.''

Gillian swallowed.

''And of course once I was here,'' Phillip continued in a smug voice that literally made her skin crawl, ''I wondered how long it would take you to figure out and find me, too.''

Too long, obviously, Gillian thought. She kept her eyes level on his, and her hand on the loaded gun hidden in the folds of her Western skirt. "I take it you've been hiding out here all morning?" she asked casually.

He gauged the odds and shrugged. "Longer than that. Ever since I left the dining hall last night."

Gillian flushed as she realized her suspicions had been on target after all. "So you were there."

"I had to make sure it was you. As soon as I saw those handwritten notes in the margin of those cookbooks, I knew. Just as you apparently knew, from the *USA Daily* article on the Net, that I only had two places to look for you and your beloved, if I didn't want to ask a lot of questions and draw attention to myself—your workplace, and his."

And since Max had placed a message on Cisco's answering machine telling clients Cisco and his secretary were on vacation for the next two weeks, Phillip had known the building would be deserted, Gillian realized, feeling ill.

Phillip started for her, a malicious glint in his dark eyes. Gillian lifted the gun and pointed it at her crazed ex-husband. "Don't come any closer."

He sized her up unpleasantly. "Since when do you carry a firearm?"

"Since I learned how to defend myself," Gillian told him flatly, letting her glance turn as menacing as his. She cocked the trigger. *"Sit down, Phillip. Now."*

His eyes still on hers, he eased obediently back into

the chair behind Cisco's desk. "And keep your hands up where I can see them," Gillian instructed.

"Or what? You'll shoot me?" Phillip mocked, unimpressed.

Gillian set her chin determinedly. "If I have to, I will."

"I don't believe it." He regarded her, hate in his eyes.

"Believe it," Gillian repeated in a cold, hard tone. Keeping a close watch on him, she ordered, "Now pick up the phone and dial 911."

"The police again, Meg? I thought we had made it clear that getting the police involved only means I'll have to beat you all the harder when they leave."

Her mouth going dry at the memory of him doing just that, Gillian ignored the icy shiver of fear moving across her skin and continued to regard him with deadly intent. "Just do it," she ordered grimly. "And keep your other hand beside your head, where I can see it."

"Fine." Phillip reached for the phone, but at the last second picked up a heavy brass paperweight and hurled it at her instead. She deftly stepped aside as it smashed against the wall.

"You'll have to kill me to get rid of me, Meg," Phillip vowed as he lurched out of the chair and kept coming. "Because this time I am not letting you go, not ever again."

Gillian knew it was him or her, and it was not going to be her—not this time. The bile rising in her throat, she took aim and fired. The months of target practice paid off because even with her hands shaking nearly uncontrollably, the bullet hit him squarely in the shoulder, several inches above his heart. Shock and disbelief spreading across his face, Phillip reeled backward and slumped against the bookcases as blood seeped through his shirt, and the acrid smell of gunpowder hung in the air.

Still keeping the gun trained on him, Gillian grabbed the phone with a shaking hand, dragged it across the desk toward her and punched in 911 herself. One way or another this was all going to end. "This is Gillian Taylor. Get Sheriff Anderson and an ambulance to Cisco Kidd's law office. I've just shot my ex-husband." She paused. "Yes, he's still alive." But the way he was bleeding, she did not know how long that would be the case. Damn it all, she thought, furious and distressed, she had never wanted to kill him, never wanted to kill anyone.

Hand pressed to his shoulder, disbelief etched on his face, Phillip staggered to his feet. "Got to…stop the bleeding…" he rasped in shock as her hands shook all the more. Heaven help her, she did not want to shoot Phillip again, but she would if it came down to it. She was not going to let him hurt her again. She was not going to let him hurt *anyone*.

"Whatever you do, don't hang up the phone," the 911 operator said.

"I won't," Gillian promised.

"Help'll be there shortly."

But what did she do until then? Gillian wondered. Swaying, Phillip grabbed on to the edge of the desk. "Meg, help me—" he moaned and then slumped facedown on the Persian carpet.

Gillian waited and waited. Still, he didn't move. Didn't take in even one, shuddering pain-filled breath.

"Oh, God," Gillian whispered hoarsely into the phone, beginning to go into shock herself. "I think I killed him."

"He may have just passed out," the 911 operator said. "Check for a pulse. Stop the bleeding if you can."

With effort, Gillian shook off the lethargy engulfing her and forced her legs to move. Still clutching the gun, she knelt beside Phillip and tried to turn him. But he was as still and heavy as a stone, and one hand wouldn't do it.

Reluctantly she put the gun to the left of her, and reached both hands out again. Calling on all her strength, she turned her ex-husband so he was lying on his back, then pressed both hands, one on top of another, to the wound in his shoulder. It seemed an eternity before the bleeding slowed, then stopped.

Knowing he was still unconscious, knowing she needed some kind of bandage to keep the wound stable, Gillian pushed numbly to her feet and went into the coffee room between the reception area and Cisco's office. She snatched a stack of soft cotton dish towels from the linen shelf. Returning, she folded one over Phillip's wound, and knotted two others together to form a sling to hold it in place.

The next thing Gillian knew, Phillip's eyes were open. The gun was in his right hand and jabbed against her throat. "Good job," Phillip rasped, as the breath left her body in one terrifying whoosh. "Now help me up."

If I go with him, I'm dead.

Gillian shook her head and, ignoring the gun pressed into her throat, pretended concern for his wound. "I think it'd be better not to move you," she said, stunned she could sound so calm when her entire universe was falling apart. "We should wait for the ambulance." *And the sheriff.*

Phillip grabbed her arm with his free hand. "Like hell we will," he grunted. "We're getting out of here, now."

She knew that voice. There was no arguing with him. No reasoning. No pleasing.

Maybe standing will make him pass out, Gillian thought, as she called on all her strength to lift him to a sitting position as rapidly as possible.

His expression turned ugly, menacing. His grip on her arm tightened brutally as he rested for a moment before lumbering to his feet. With an anguished gasp, he held the gun to her neck and half dragged, half pushed her to walk backward to the door. "You never should have tried to fool me, Meg."

"I wanted to end the violence."

Sweat dripped off his chin and onto her forehead as he forced her to keep moving again. "Of course, what you never understood, Meg, was that our committment to each other was a lifelong affair," he informed her coldly.

No, my love for Cisco is a lifelong affair, Gillian

thought, realizing that because of her attempts to spare Cisco and his family any danger, by bringing it all on herself, that it might be too late for her and Cisco after all.

"Not that I didn't try to teach you," Phillip lamented in a sick, vicious voice that chilled her to her soul. Shaking his head, he pushed her through the library. "I tried everything I knew to show you how to be a good, obedient wife—"

"But I just couldn't learn, could I?" Gillian countered sarcastically, her heartbeat picking up frantically as he shoved her out of the law office, toward Cisco's car. "And now you've got an even bigger problem," Gillian said, struggling and digging in her heels, despite the gun pointed at her throat. "Because Cisco and the whole McKendrick family are going to know that you've done this and they're not going to rest until they see that you get what you have coming to you."

"And what is that, Meg?" Phillip took hold of her hair and jerked her face up to his. "What do I have coming to me?" Phillip echoed with a violent sarcasm that made her shiver. "You?"

"No," Cisco said, stepping from around the side of the office building. "This is what you have coming to you." He cocked his rifle, an expression of lethal seriousness on his face. There was no doubt in anyone's mind that he would not hesitate to shoot. "Let her go, Phillip."

"So you can have her?" Phillip jerked Gillian in

front of him and gave her hair a vicious yank that made her cry out in pain. "I don't think so."

Trace, Max and Cody all stepped forward. All were armed. And so was Sheriff Anderson. "You're surrounded, Wingate. You don't have a chance. Drop your weapon and let the girl go—now," Sheriff Anderson ordered.

Knowing if she miscalculated she'd likely end up dead, and if she did nothing to stop him now she'd also likely end up dead, Gillian put her foot back and hooked it behind one of his at the same time she gave him two hard elbows, one low to his ribs, the other high to his wound.

As she had hoped, Phillip winced in pain and lost his footing. His grip on her loosening, he stumbled backward, swearing.

Gasping in terror, Gillian pushed away from Phillip and the wildly waving gun with all her might. She dove headfirst for the ground, hitting it hard enough to knock the wind right out of her just as the gun in Phillip's hand discharged.

The silence that followed was deafening. But no more shots followed. None were necessary. Phillip was utterly still, felled by the gun in his own hand. Sheriff Anderson sprang into action as the paramedics and other officers arrived, but in the end there was not much they could do.

Her knees shaking so badly, they felt as if they would no longer support her, Gillian turned to Cisco, wanting only him.

His eyes locked with hers emotionally. He crossed

to her side, gathered her close and kissed her with a rough possessiveness that shook her to her very soul.

"I'm sorry," she said when the stormy kiss had ended, able to see and feel how he had suffered, seeing her in such danger. "I should have told you, I should have let you come with me!"

"You ought to be sorry," Cisco chastised hotly, scowling down at her as a muscle worked convulsively in his jaw. "Damn it all, Gillian. You could have been killed!"

Chapter Twelve

"Okay, just say it, and get it over with," Gillian urged Cisco wearily the moment they walked in the door to the honeymoon cottage.

Cisco stiffened and cursed softly under his breath, aware she wasn't the only one who couldn't bear this tension between them much longer. "Say what?" he demanded gruffly.

Gillian sighed and continued trying to decipher the expression in his dark gray eyes. She couldn't read it and she didn't like this situation.

Was he through with her because of what she'd done? Still in it for the inheritance? Or planning to inherit and then ever so gently and gallantly cut her loose from this marriage they still found themselves in? She didn't know the answer. She only knew that, deep down, he was hurting—and yes, probably as confused—as she.

"You're still mad as heck with me for leaving and going off alone, aren't you?" she guessed finally when the continuing silence between them nearly un-did her.

Cisco shrugged impassively as he hung his cowboy hat on the hook by the back door and tossed his keys onto the kitchen counter.

"What, in all of Montana, would make you think that?" he countered emotionlessly, looping his thumbs through his belt and adapting a censuring, spread-legged stance.

"Oh, gee, I don't know," Gillian replied, aware his anger and disappointment had kindled her own. "Maybe the fact that although you stood stoically by me during the entire police investigation into Phillip's death as any good husband or attorney would, and Max and the McKendricks obviously wanted you to, you haven't said much of anything to me personally, not then, and not on the ride back to the cottage."

"What's there to say?" Cisco asked with as much indifference as he could muster as he kept his eyes on hers. He hated the self-doubt her actions had en-gendered in him. "You didn't trust me to be able to protect you, so instead of confiding in me and letting me know straight out that you thought Phillip was in town, instead of giving me a chance to be the kind of husband you needed and wanted, you staged that whole elaborate kiss-off. Then you ditched me the first chance you got and put your own life in danger, without any thought to yourself or me or the rest of the McKendricks or how we'd feel if anything hap-pened to you." In his view, those actions pretty much spoke for themselves.

Gillian's green eyes gleamed with moisture. She walked toward him, hands outstretched. "I was trying to spare you any further hurt," she explained.

Cisco scowled and shook his head. He couldn't believe he had let himself be this vulnerable to a woman, never mind one as distrusting of him as Gillian Taylor.

"Yeah, well, you didn't," he shot back roughly, shoving a hand through his hair. "Although I have to admit that knowing your past, and knowing what you'd said earlier, I had half expected you to run out on me and our marriage the first chance you got, on whatever flimsy excuse presented itself to you. But like a fool I hoped the intimacy we had shared the past two days would have bound you to me, and made you have second thoughts." He had hoped, in short, for a miracle that was never going to happen.

Gillian gaped at him, furious. "Maybe I made a mistake in going off alone, I'll grant you that, but I did not use Phillip's presence as a handy excuse to run away from our marriage, Cisco! I did it for a lot of reasons."

"Such as—?"

"I wanted Max and you and the rest of the family to be able to go ahead with the profile in *Personalities!* magazine. That wasn't going to be possible if I stayed here."

Cisco regarded her incredulously.

Gillian glared right back at him. "You're determined to stay angry with me, aren't you?"

"I don't want to feel this way," Cisco retorted,

able to feel the tension coming off her in waves. "The fact is, Phillip's threat to you was something we should have handled together, Gillian. Not just in the beginning, when you finally confided in me and we brought Sheriff Anderson and the rest of the family in to help us deal with the situation, but the entire time. The fact that you instead chose to go it alone once again as soon as the going got really rough, says a lot about your lack of faith and trust in me, doesn't it?"

And damn it all to hell, he hated this feeling that he had failed to be what she wanted and needed…in the same way he had failed to be the child the foster parents had wanted and needed. Cisco turned away, aware his heart and soul had never felt heavier.

"I want a woman I can trust, and a marriage I can rely on." At the moment, he didn't feel he had either in Gillian.

The tears that had been gathering in her eyes rolled down her cheeks. Stubbornly she rubbed them away and moved closer, in a drift of hyacinth perfume. "I thought you'd understand I was just doing what was best, in doing what I had to do alone."

Cisco knew she'd never consciously set out to hurt him, but that knowledge only made things worse. "That's the problem, Gillian. I do understand," Cisco said sadly. "When you acted the way you did, you were just following your heart, just as Max advised." He shook his head in exasperation, aware he had never been more involved with a woman or given more of himself. And yet it had all turned out wrong anyway. He sighed. "I love Max, and God knows you're right," Cisco continued, his lips set grimly. "I'd do just about anything for him. But it was a stupid idea to try and tie two complete strangers together in forty-eight hours or less." Worse, Cisco felt like an utter fool for buying into it. For allowing himself to think that two days and nights of passion could lead to an entire lifetime of the same.

Gillian didn't love him.

For a time she had needed him, to give her a new identity and a permanent home and family on the ranch, but now that need did not even remain. Because the McKendricks were not going to desert her, any more than they had deserted him.

"What are you trying to tell me?" Gillian demanded, coming closer. She released a long, impatient breath. "That you no longer want your inheritance from Max?"

Cisco turned to Gillian and regarded her quietly. He wished he still did not find her so beautiful, with her wildly curling auburn hair, fair skin and dark green eyes. He wished he still did not want to make love to her with every fiber of his being. But he did, and he sensed that would never change, either, no matter how long—or how far—they were apart.

Nevertheless, he had to be practical.

He had to end the hurt, and crushed dreams, and get past her guilt over hurting him, and help them both move on to greener pastures.

"My inheritance I figure I've earned," he told Gillian gruffly. "But as for the rest of it..." He shrugged. "Like you said earlier, it was a nice romance while it lasted, but that's all it ever was or will be, so I suggest we do ourselves a favor, and just call it quits as soon as our forty-eight hours together are over."

Gillian stared at him, behaving as if she could hardly believe her ears. "Fine," she said quietly, holding her hands in a gesture of surrender, letting him know in a glance it was over between them as far as she was concerned, too. "If that's what you want," she finished coldly, "then that's what we'll do."

"I THOUGHT I USED TO BE all business before Susannah came back into my life, but this really takes the cake. I can't believe you're sitting here doing paperwork when you and Gillian are both going to be officially declared McKendricks in a few hours," Trace told Cisco when he and Susannah had dropped by the cottage to check on them and see how they were doing.

Cisco shrugged. "Gillian has decided to keep the false name she's been going by for the past ten years, and just add the McKendrick on at the end. That means there are papers to be filled out. Fortunately, the judge Max asked to preside over the wedding ceremony is a personal friend of mine, and after hearing the extenuating circumstances, he has agreed to rule on our petition to have Gillian legally change her name to Gillian Taylor McKendrick and revert back to the Social Security number she was assigned at birth, at the same time Max officially adopts me as his son.''

Trace settled in a wing chair next to the living room fireplace. ''Bet straightening that out with the Social Security Administration and the IRS won't be easy,'' he commiserated with Cisco ruefully.

And yet it had to be easier than leaving her, Cisco thought. Because even knowing what he did about Gillian, and the way she had run out on him the first chance she got, he was sorely tempted—though not foolish enough—to give her a second chance. There were, after all, only so many times a man could put his heart and soul on the line and set himself up for rejection.

''I'm sure it can be taken care of,'' Cisco replied smoothly as he finished typing the documents on the laptop computer he had retrieved from his office before heading out to the cottage. Satisfied all was as it should be, he copied the documents onto a diskette for safekeeping.

''What about the rest of it?'' Trace asked.

Cisco typed in a command, and reached over to turn his portable ink-jet printer on.

''The important part,'' Trace continued. ''Your relationship with Gillian.''

''We're working things out on a businesslike level,'' Cisco said.

''Businesslike!'' Trace echoed, incredulous.

Cisco nodded and continued matter-of-factly. ''We've agreed to stay married and under the same roof as long as Max deems suitable to collect our inheritances. But that's as far as it goes."

Trace looked all the more upset. "Cisco, you can't run a marriage like a business deal." He leaned forward earnestly. "It doesn't work. That's why Susannah and I got divorced the first time around."

Cisco removed the printed pages from the laser-jet, examined them for accuracy, then switched off the printer. "Your situation was different. You and Susannah loved each other."

"From what I saw earlier, when you were half out of your mind with worry over Gillian, when she struck out on her own and put her own life in danger rather than continue to put you at risk, you two loved each other, too," Trace said meaningfully.

Cisco pushed aside his deep disappointment as he cut the power to his computer with a decisive snap. "Appearances can be deceiving."

"Meaning?"

Cisco unplugged both his printer and computer. He met Trace's glance, man-to-man. "I know Gillian never *meant* to hurt me. That goes without saying. But I need someone in my life I can count on. Someone I know won't run away, no matter how rough the going gets." And sad to say, Cisco thought wearily, that just wasn't Gillian.

Trace sighed, looking very much like the older brother he had become to Cisco. "Your mind's made up, then?" Trace queried, clearly disappointed in the way things were working out for the last of Max's heirs. "You won't give her a second chance?"

Cisco shrugged, aware he'd never felt more disillusioned or letdown in his entire life. He'd tried to be everything Gillian needed in a husband and a lover and he'd failed miserably, otherwise she wouldn't have left. Determined to cut his losses while he still could, he shrugged dispiritedly. "What would be the point?"

"YOU PUT ME through agony this morning, running off that way," Susannah said, sitting opposite Gillian in the cottage kitchen. "When Trace and I got word from Cisco...well, let's just say we both nearly went out of our mind with worry. And what we felt was nothing to what Cisco was going through."

"I'm sorry I upset all of you," Gillian said. She took one set of blueberry muffins out of the oven, and put in a batch of bittersweet chocolate brownies. Gillian straightened and wiped her brow, continuing numbly, "I'm sorry I upset everyone."

Including Cisco. Especially Cisco. She should have known he wouldn't forgive her for lying to him and trying to handle everything alone. But she had to confront her past...alone.

"Shouldn't you be getting ready for the party Max is throwing for the two of you this evening?" Susannah asked.

Gillian shrugged. Although she was happy Cisco's adoption was going to be made official that evening, as was her legal name change, the way she looked for the important family gathering was the last thing on her mind. Besides, she'd already had a long shower and washed her hair. "I've got plenty of time yet." She began preparing another batch of dough.

Susannah studied her thoughtfully. "Oh, no, Gillian. Don't tell me you're having second thoughts about continuing your marriage to Cisco."

"Okay, I won't tell you."

Susannah's eyes widened. "Gillian!" she reprimanded.

Gillian, not about to be swayed by any sentimental arguments, held up a flour-dusted palm, staving off further lectures on the subject of her soon-to-be exhusband. "Hey. If it were up to me...if I wouldn't be costing Cisco his inheritance, I would just take off and head back to California right this instant," she declared emphatically. After all, this wasn't the first disappointment she'd weathered. Nor was it likely to be her last. So what if this just happened to be a soul-crushing one? So what if her heart was breaking?

Susannah sighed like the incurable romantic she was, looking not the least bit ready to give up on them. "So what's going on? Are the two of you fighting?"

"I wouldn't exactly call it that," she hedged, reluctant to confess any more, for fear she'd give away how completely her heart was breaking.

Susannah's eyes narrowed. "Then what would you call it?" she persisted seriously.

"A complete and utter breakdown in communications," Gillian said finally. "A case of the knight in shining armor needing to move on to the next damsel in distress."

"Oh, Gillian," her old friend lamented softly. "Trace and I were so hoping you and Cisco would overlook the unusual way your romance began and decide to stay married past the forty-eight-hour stipulation."

"I know." Gillian forced a wan smile as she felt all her dreams slipping away from her at once. She put the half-finished dough back into a ceramic bowl to rest. "But we have to face it, Susannah. Despite the fact Cisco and I make a handsome couple, despite the chemistry—and I'll be the first to admit there is plenty of that... " *Or at least there used to be*, she amended silently, *before I struck out on my own and let him down in a way he just can't forgive.* "Whether or not you and I like it or not...Cisco and I just weren't meant to be."

AT SIX O'CLOCK that evening, the caravan began coming up the drive. Cisco and Gillian stood watching in the windows as one Silver Spur Ranch vehicle after another parked in front of the honeymoon cottage. As the family members began piling out of their vehicles, Cisco turned to Gillian, his expression every bit as dismal and reluctant as hers. "The judge who is going to handle the adoption and name changes will be here in another hour to handle the formalities," he reminded her. "Max also has another attorney coming to hand over our inheritances."

Gillian's shoulders stiffened. "I know."

"Meanwhile, I suppose we should go out together and greet the family."

Gillian drew a bracing breath and turned to face Cisco. She hadn't expected leaving him to be so hard, but it was.

"You're sure you want to do this as a couple," she asked softly, thinking maybe it was time the charade came to an end. Especially since the McKendricks were all pushing hard for her and Cisco to make their marriage a permanent one despite the problems, and wouldn't hesitate to lobby hard for just that.

Cisco shrugged and glanced out at the catered party being assembled on the lawn. "I'd rather delay going out there until the very last moment, but I know how their minds work when it comes to us and the sparks between us. If we don't go out there together, promptly, they'll probably think they've interrupted something, by showing up early."

Gillian rolled her eyes. Cisco had not come near her since they'd returned from town. Ignoring her disappointment, she told herself she preferred it that way.

"Not much chance of that," she said.

His mouth curved into a bittersweet grimace as he met her eyes. "No, there isn't, is there?" he replied.

Silence fell between them, a silence Gillian had no clue how to bridge. "In that case…" Gillian sighed dispiritedly, aware her heart was breaking like never before. But it was her fault; she'd set herself up for this disappointment by allowing herself to believe their spur-of-the-moment marriage actually had a chance! "I guess you're right. We should get this party rolling and go out and say hello."

"Wise decision." Cisco gestured stiffly, letting her know she should go first.

"Well, what's the verdict for you two lovebirds?" Pearl demanded the moment Gillian and Cisco were through the door.

"Yeah," Susannah and Trace's four rambunctious sons blurted out in unison. "Are you two staying together or aren't you?"

Gillian looked at Cisco. He looked back at her. There was no denying this was it, the moment of truth. With the entire McKendrick family waiting to hear the mutual declarations of love she and Cisco had never expressed, Gillian did not know what to say.

She just knew she didn't want her love affair with Cisco to end, any more than she wanted their marriage to continue just so they could inherit from Max.

She swallowed, still studying him, gauging his reaction to the quandary they were in. "Well, boys, that's a good question—" Gillian started nervously.

"And one we haven't finished discussing," Cisco interrupted firmly before she could get another word in edgewise. "So if you all will excuse us, Gillian and I are going to take a few moments to do just that."

Gillian turned to him, hands on her hips. How like him, she thought irately, to make a unilateral decision for both of them. "Says who?" she demanded hotly.

"Says me," Cisco growled as the whole family hooted and hollered their encouragement for such a daring, romantic deed.

Before she could say another word, Cisco swept her up into his arms. Looking and acting more than ever like a real McKendrick, he carried her over the threshold and into the cottage, kicking the door shut behind him.

"Okay, Counselor, the show's over. You can put me down now," Gillian said as soon as they were out of earshot of the others.

Tightening his grip on her possessively, Cisco continued on up the stairs to their bedroom on the second floor. "Not a chance."

Gillian wreathed her arms about his neck and let her pride shield her broken heart. "I don't know what you're thinking!"

He paused to give her a dark, dangerous look. "Don't you," he said softly.

Gillian gulped as he swept through the bedroom door. "No."

He set her down gently next to the bed. "I think it's time we called off the war of wills going on between us and followed through on what we started two days ago."

He made it sound as simple as concluding a business deal, and this wasn't! "Look, Cisco," Gillian began, feeling utterly exasperated even as her hopes were born again. "I know I promised you I'd hang around to see this marriage through to the end of the forty-eight hours—"

"Yes, you did," Cisco agreed sternly, his expression both tender and determined. "And I've decided I'm going to hold you to that promise, Gillian."

"—but I've had a change of heart," Gillian continued, pretending he hadn't spoken. "I am *not* going to stay married to you just because it's what everyone else in the family seems to want!" Gillian folded her arms in front of her.

"Then do it because you want to," Cisco pleaded with her in a voice that was husky with regret. Looking as though he had never wanted her more in his life, he sat down on the bed, hooked a hand around her waist and pulled her down to sit on his lap. "Do it because you know we belong together, not just for a wild fling or a few days and nights, but for the rest of our lives."

Gillian's whole body tensed. So much was at stake. "Is that the way you feel?" Was he trying to tell her, in a roundabout way, that he might just love her? The way she already knew she loved him?

In answer, he bent to kiss her on the lips, sweetly, lingeringly. "You're the only woman for me, Gillian," he murmured as his hands pressed her intimately close, until there was nothing between them but unspoken love and hot burning need. "The only woman there'll ever be."

His heartfelt admission was both balm for her soul and hope for their future. "Oh, Cisco, I feel that way about us, too," Gillian declared softly, exalting in the words of genuine commitment she had so longed for him to speak and feared she might never hear.

"Glad to hear it." He pressed a kiss to her temple. "But I need to know what changed your mind," she whispered emotionally as she settled more comfortably on his lap.

Cisco tightened his hold on her. "It's what Max said to us when this whole thing started, about listening to our hearts," he confessed huskily, his eyes darkening with emotion. "My heart is telling me to forget the mischievous way we were goaded into this marriage and the agreement we had to end it before we even gave it a chance." He paused, his expression serious as he caught her hand and lifted it to his lips. He kissed her fingers one by one. "I know what I led you to believe, but it was never the inheritance that I wanted, Gillian. It was you. It was everything we've shared and everything we could have if only we stick it out long enough to make things right between us. And they could be right, Gillian, right enough to make it over the long haul, if we just give us a chance."

"Oh, Cisco, I am willing to do that."

"So am I."

Gillian breathed a sigh of relief as she wrapped her arms around him and held him tightly. "It's funny," she confessed, long moments later as they continued to hold each other, as the party preparations continued outside. "At first I was worried about you only wanting to be with me because of the inheritance, and your penchant for helping damsels in distress. Then I thought it was the passion keeping us together. But now that you've told me how you feel I really do think we can make this work."

Cisco smiled down at her confidently and stroked

a hand through her hair. "We have a lot in common, Gillian."

She looked at him, already knowing, in her heart, their feelings for each other were strong enough to last a lifetime.

But the woman in her wanted to hear him tell her why. "Such as—?" she prodded gently.

Cisco shrugged his shoulders negligently and he leaned forward to give her a sensual, lingering kiss. "Neither of us likes to be told what to do or to be stuck in a situation."

Gillian sighed contentedly and looked into his ruggedly handsome face. He knew her so well! "How right you are about that!" she teased.

His pewter eyes darkened seriously as he drew back. "And we both know what it's like to be without family, and to yearn for that with all our hearts, even while we practically move heaven and earth to keep people from hurting us again."

"Or getting close to us at all," Gillian said sadly.

Cisco nodded as he stroked his hand down her arm. "But when Max threw us together the way he did…all that began to change. And it was more than just the circumstances drawing us together," he told her confidently, pausing to kiss her once again.

"It was fate. And chemistry and destiny," Gillian continued as they drew apart, knowing she had never been happier or more content than she was at that very moment.

"And love," Cisco added emotionally, as he

stroked a hand through her hair. "Love unlike anything I have ever or will ever feel again."

"For me, too," Gillian whispered as her heart filled
with joy and tears of happiness misted her eyes. "Because I do love you," she continued huskily, "with
all my heart and soul."

Cisco framed her face with his hand, tilting her face
up to his, and kissed her hard, stamping her as his.
"Stay married to me, Gillian," he urged as their kiss
deepened and warmed. "But this time do it for all the
right reasons. Because you love me as much as I love
you and because you want to build a life together,
and have a home and family together, too."

"I do," Gillian whispered, kissing him back
fiercely. "Oh, Cisco, I do, I do!"

GILLIAN AND CISCO SHARED their happy news with
the family at sunset. Their announcement was met
with hearty congratulations and plenty of well wishes.
A beaming Max signed over their inheritances, Cisco
officially became Max's son and Gillian and Cisco
both legally became McKendricks, too.

It was a lot to celebrate, and afterward, as Gillian
and Cisco both expected, quite a party broke out. And
it was during the dancing, that Gillian first spied the
gold band and diamond solitaire sparkling on the ring
finger of Pearl's left hand. Gillian nudged her husband, wanting him to see. Grinning, she and Cisco
danced closer. "Pearl, is that a wedding ring on your
finger?" Gillian demanded.

Pearl grinned proudly. "It sure is."

"What changed your mind?" Cisco asked.

Pearl cast Max a dreamy look. "Two things. First, I realized how much Max loved me and always had. And second, I found out about the plans he'd had for the two of us all along."

"I was aiming to ask Pearl to marry me as soon as I had all four of you kids and your spouses hitched and settled in," Max explained.

"He didn't want anything interfering with the romantic plans he had for our I Do's," Pearl confided.

"But unfortunately," Max added, possessively tightening his hold on his new wife, "Pearl never gave me a chance to follow through on the surprise I was planning just for her after the quadruple wedding ceremony had ended."

"Instead, I left the reception altogether," Pearl reminded as Cisco and Gillian both recalled.

"So," Max said with a sigh, "I decided to wait it out a day or so—until this woman of mine was calm enough to really listen to the very important words I had to say to her—and then I took her to Silver Mountain for a romantic, candlelit dinner of our very own."

"Where he showed me the site he'd picked out for our new home on the ranch and proposed to me right there, under the stars." Pearl smiled.

"Naturally," Max grinned, too, "she said yes. And the preacher who married the rest of you young'uns led us through our vows."

Pearl lifted her index finger to her lips. "But now! We don't want the word about our elopement getting out until *after* our honeymoon."

"Which is going to be where?" Gillian whispered, feeling delighted but not all that surprised the two had finally gotten together and made it official. Like herself and Cisco, she'd had the feeling Pearl and Max were just meant to be together.

Max inclined his head at the deluxe silver recreational vehicle coming up the drive. "Wherever our hearts and fancies take us," he said.

"But don't you worry." Pearl smiled, as she laid her face against Max's shoulder contentedly. "We'll be back."

Max nodded. "Retired or not, we intend to be around, conquering new vistas—"

"—and matchmaking for this family," Pearl added.

"—for years to come."

THE GUESTS HAD all departed by midnight. Cisco Kidd McKendrick put a bottle of champagne on ice, while Gillian Taylor McKendrick turned down the covers. They changed into matching silk robes and met upstairs on the bed. Cisco poured them each a glass of the golden liquor and offered the first toast. "To a long and happy life together, Mrs. McKendrick," he said as they settled comfortably against the pillows.

They clinked glasses, locked arms, sipped and kissed.

"To a long and happy life and plenty of children," Gillian wished, in a voice filled with love and tenderness.

Cisco touched the rim of his glass to hers. All the love he felt for her was in his eyes. "I could go for that," he murmured sexily.

Gillian put her glass—and his—aside and slid into his arms. It was amazing, but all her dreams had come true. And in just forty-eight hours! "Well, in that case," she teased, deftly untying the belt on his robe, "how 'bout we just get started on that right now."

His grin as wide as all Montana, Cisco reached for her and pulled her so close, they could feel their hearts beating in tandem. He framed her face with his hands and kissed her until they trembled. "You bet."

Take 4 bestselling love stories FREE

Plus get a FREE surprise gift!

Special Limited-time Offer

Mail to Harlequin Reader Service®

3010 Walden Avenue
P.O. Box 1867
Buffalo, N.Y. 14240-1867

YES! Please send me 4 free Harlequin American Romance® novels and my free surprise gift. Then send me 4 brand-new novels every month, which I will receive months before they appear in bookstores. Bill me at the low price of $3.12 each plus 25¢ delivery and applicable sales tax, if any.* That's the complete price and a savings of over 10% off the cover prices—quite a bargain! I understand that accepting the books and gift places me under no obligation ever to buy any books. I can always return a shipment and cancel at any time. Even if I never buy another book from Harlequin, the 4 free books and the surprise gift are mine to keep forever.

154 BPA A3UM

Name _____
                          (PLEASE PRINT)

Address _____ Apt. No. _____

City _____ State _____ Zip _____

This offer is limited to one order per household and not valid to present Harlequin American Romance® subscribers. *Terms and prices are subject to change without notice. Sales tax applicable in N.Y.

HARLEQUIN®
AMERICAN ✦ ROMANCE®

You asked for it…You got it! More MEN!

MORE THAN MEN

We're thrilled to bring you another special edition of the
popular MORE THAN MEN series—and thrilled
to bring you another unique book by the inimitable,
RITA Award-winning author Anne Stuart.

Like those who have come before him, O'Neal is more
than tall, dark and handsome. All of these men have
extraordinary powers that make them "more than men."
But whether they're able to grant you three wishes, or live
forever, make no mistake—their greatest, most extraordinary
power is that of seduction.

So make a date with O'Neal in…

#702 A DARK & STORMY NIGHT
by Anne Stuart
November 1997

MEN1197

As Seen on TV!

Free Gift Offer

With a Free Gift proof-of-purchase
from any Harlequin® book, you can receive
a beautiful cubic zirconia pendant.

This stunning marquise-shaped stone is a genuine cubic
zirconia—accented by an 18" gold tone necklace.
(Approximate retail value $19.95)

Send for yours today...
compliments of ✦HARLEQUIN®

To receive your free gift, a cubic zirconia pendant, send us one original proof-of-purchase, photocopies not accepted, from the back of any Harlequin Romance®, Harlequin Presents®, Harlequin Temptation®, Harlequin Superromance®, Harlequin Intrigue®, Harlequin American Romance®, or Harlequin Historicals® title available at your favorite retail outlet, together with the Free Gift Certificate, plus a check or money order for $1.65 U.S./$2.15 CAN. (do not send cash) to cover postage and handling, payable to Harlequin Free Gift Offer. We will send you the specified gift. Allow 6 to 8 weeks for delivery. Offer good until December 31, 1997, or while quantities last. Offer valid in the U.S. and Canada only.

Free Gift Certificate

Name: _____

Address: _____

City: _____ State/Province: _____ Zip/Postal Code: _____

Mail this certificate, one proof-of-purchase and a check or money order for postage and handling to: HARLEQUIN FREE GIFT OFFER 1997. In the U.S.: 3010 Walden Avenue, P.O. Box 9071, Buffalo NY 14269-9057. In Canada: P.O. Box 604, Fort Erie, Ontario L2Z 5X3.

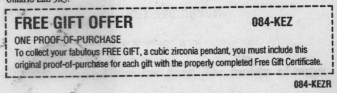

FREE GIFT OFFER   084-KEZ
ONE PROOF-OF-PURCHASE
To collect your fabulous FREE GIFT, a cubic zirconia pendant, you must include this original proof-of-purchase for each gift with the properly completed Free Gift Certificate.

084-KEZR